i

Narratives From The Lockdown

The Second Wave

Narratives From The Lockdown

The Second Wave

G G Howells

Dedicated to the memory of a

great man.

My mate, Ralph.

Contents

Brave New Normal

Three months had passed, and we had already become used to and accepted so much as our current reality.

I took my usual evening walk around the lake in the diminishing light of sunset. Just before the darkness began to envelope the landscape; the reddish hue of the last of the evening light bathed the wild and untamed weeds that now thrived along the length and breadth of every street, briefly making my surroundings eerily resemble the weird and lurid landscape of another planet; as though the conditions which give Mars its red appearance had manifested here on Earth.

As daylight began dimming to black, I was usually left with an overbearing sense of despair and loneliness, hanging in the air. This evening was no different.

Many people's lives had fundamentally changed. People had faced tragedy and loss. Many had not been afforded the opportunity to confront and process down their pain, given the many restrictions.

Some had not reacted well to the enforced societal divisions and had cut themselves off from all personal relationships that they had spent years, even decades, constructing and nurturing, withdrawing deep within themselves in some cases.

In the first few weeks, friends and family members alike swore that they would all make an extra effort to ensure that they did not become estranged from one another during these 'unprecedented' times. I was not alone in downloading a new app to my phone that would allow me and several friends to all virtually meet up, and then simultaneously talk loudly over the top of one another whilst our individual video tiles were arranged into a grid on the screen like an episode of 'Celebrity Squares'. Only this was an episode where you recognised everyone.

After the initial novelty value had worn off, it just became annoying and my friends and I resorted back to using messaging services – and I know we were not alone. It did, however, strike me as fitting that whilst we were all flirting with life in 'The New Normal', we should begin by communicating with each through a medium that made it look as though my friends were trapped in some virtual version of 'The Upside Down'. The black background that swarmed and surrounded their personal video tile like a penetrative black fog – giving these interactions an other-worldly quality.

This new generational sub-header of 'The New Normal' felt disingenuous, and I didn't approve at all. Things that had the prefix of 'The New...' suggested something fresh and exciting and acted as a watershed before better times were set to commence. The most prominent example perhaps being 'The New Deal'.

What we were faced with now did not rank up there with 'The New Deal', which was a series of programs, public work projects, regulations and financial reforms enacted by Franklin Delano Roosevelt (32nd President of the United States) to provide relief, reform and recovery following the Great Depression – the worst economic crisis in American history. This initiative had brought relief to millions of

Americans who had suffered relentless economic hardship for years.

It didn't hold a candle to 'The New Testament' either. Whilst the Old Testament contained some of the greatest hits – many of the crowd-pleasing stories about Adam and Eve, Noah's Ark, or David and Goliath, for example - in essence, it had collected the sacred scriptures of the Jewish faith. The New Testament – which was surely the most difficult of all second albums – was full of more modern stories about the life and times of Jesus and all of his hip, enlightened pals – which provided a more practicable and useful means of trying to achieve human fulfilment and bettering the world one lives in, even if it could be accused of pandering to new trends.

As a further contrast, the God of the Old Testament was a wrathful, judgemental, unforgiving, jealous deity. The God of the New Testament – incarnated as Jesus Christ – was an infinitely more chilled out and understanding dude. And it is the more revolutionary inclusivity of the New Testament regarding matters of race, sexuality, and gender that make it more relevant to a human being's actual life on Earth.

I'm not even sure that this 'The New Normal' is even up to taking on 'The New Romantic' movement of the early 1980's, in any conclusive manner. Whether or not the music this era ushered in is better than the music which went before – basically glam rock and the anti-fashion punk stance – is a matter of opinion. However, I am certain that were it not for the presence of David Bowie as one of its leading protagonists, then it may not be a close run thing.

One thing was certain. The impending era of 'The New Normal' was of considerable cause for concern. Just six months earlier, no one would have believed that in what were the early years of the 21st Century, human affairs could be so heavily impacted by microscopic invaders that could multiply with so much as a cough, or the briefest of contact.

Six months earlier, the human race had been busying themselves with their usual brand of self-serving endeavours and had barely noticed the beginnings of the current pandemic happening across the ocean and all of its basins. Everyone carried on in blissful ignorance – not believing that this would ever affect them. Eating out, attending football matches, going to horse racing fixtures – and many other types of what we now refer to as 'mass gatherings'.

All we had now were reminders; samples of what we once enjoyed without giving it a second thought. We were being told to get back to work – but where possible people continued to work from home. Go shopping, and spend some money – but in reality, it was a dour experience of queuing outside discount sports shops and the like; online was just too easy. Eat out and you will be helping out, we were assured. Although in hindsight, there is not universal agreement as to whether this was a good call.

Initially it was enjoyable for these public places to not be crowded, but as we would find out, most restaurants or pubs at 50% capacity don't really work, and once the new normal kicked in, casualties followed. If there were to be any chance of returning to the now fetishized 'good old days', it could take a generation to pass.

I began the return leg to my abode just as the streetlights started blinking on – the few on the main road that ran through the housing estate which had already been

4

converted to LED technology for cost saving measures, that is. Turn left or right on to any street and they were basking in a dusky hue – soon to be darkness.

The weather had been typical for the end of August and served as a reminder as to how much time had passed in these shackles. The days were typically mild but with the undercurrent of a chill that told you that Summer was officially over, and Winter was bearing down on you. The chill in the evening air even more potent, and I slipped up the hood on my hoodie top.

Well apparently, it wasn't a hoodie, but merely a jacket with a hood. My wife had said that, and we had argued, but the name was still misleading in my opinion. She said it was a hooded jogging jacket, and that a true hoodie – a hoodie worth its salt – would not have a full zip and needed to be donned by putting it on over your head. It would then be sported more like a jumper, which is why I believed that we should compromise, and settle on calling it a hooded jumper.

I approached the lake on my way home. The whole area measured around five acres, in the centre of which lay the lake. Immediately encircling it was a footpath, and fifty feet away up a grassy bank, lay a further tarmacked path that also orbited the water. The inner footpath was often muddy, and so most walkers would use the upper tarmacked path. The lake was rich with life – carp, ducks, herons. A once vibrant place with swarms of people jogging around it all hours of the day and evening, lay still and noiseless.

On the far side from where I was, near the road, lay a large culvert which was framed inside a concrete wall - the top of which protruded over the grassy bank. It stood about 20 feet or so over the metal drain below it. As I got closer to it, I heard the sounds of sobbing, and a kind of incoherent mumbling emanating from behind the wall.

Approaching with caution, I softened my footsteps so as not to alert this person to my presence. I was now within ten feet of the culvert wall, and abruptly the sound ceased. I paused for a moment, standing stationary. Everything lay comatose, apart from the red weeds – their prickly tentacles swaying in the evening breeze.

Suddenly, from behind the wall, I heard a voice cut through the solitude.

"I know you're there. He told me you would come."

It was a man's voice. He was softly spoken – weak even, and undeniably agitated. He did not seem to be able to exercise any control over the pitch and tone of his voice. This incoordination of his vocal control system likely the result of muscle tension in his voice box - often brought about by considerable stress and anxiety. I maintained my guard.

"Are you ok there? Who told you that?"

I didn't get an immediate reply for what seemed like a couple of minutes. It was getting palpably darker with each passing moment. I had started to begin thinking that I had imagined the whole encounter, until –

"Who do you think? God."

God predicted my arrival? Pretty much anyone whose house I wandered past each evening could have managed it. However, I did not want to mock as the man seemed to be displaying some concerning tendencies. At this point, I still had not clapped eyes on him, so becoming confrontational and perhaps even provoking a potential physical altercation could be a bad idea.

"He did? Well, he was right – here I am! Why don't you come around from there so I can see who I am talking to?"

A moments' hesitation was followed by the sound of something snapping, like a large bolt slamming into its hole. The man yelped like a scalded dog.

I instinctively motioned to step forward, before checking myself and holding back, but craning my neck to catch sight of him.

"Mate? Are you ok?"

He panted a few times and then there was an audible murmuring - which I could not be sure was either sobbing or chuckling.

"I spent my life working for the church you know."

"Oh yeah. Are you some kind of reverend or vicar?" I replied.

I wanted to engage with the man, but I was becoming ever more convinced that his mental state could make him somewhat unpredictable. I thought about simply retreating the way I had come but had decided to not take that option just yet.

"I was a curate. An assistant to the Vicar. I'm not anymore…." His voice trailed off at the end of this sentence.

"Guess there's no congregations at the moment?" I shivered in the evening breeze.

"Not in the church. But that's not why."

As much as my curiosity had been piqued by this situation, my gut instinct was telling me I needed to leave. I was aware that I had suddenly become hyper alert as this primal wisdom suggested to me that there could be danger lurking in this scenario.

Nonetheless, I attempted to make a compassionate plea with the man.

"Come from around there and tell me what has happened."

There was another loud snap followed again by a feverish, fraught howl. This time it was unmistakeably followed up by uncontrollable sobbing. This time I froze and waited.

In between the sobbing, and the sniffing, he managed to pose a question: "What sins have we done to deserve this?"

I asked him what he meant, but it became quickly apparent that the man's grief was inconsolable.

"Why are these things permitted?"

"Permitted by whom?" I retorted.

His pace became more feverish. "This must be the beginning of the end. The End! The great and terrible day of the Lord."

I began to understand the position he was taking, and once against asked him to show himself. He did not respond to the question, instead he continued along his train of thought.

"All our work here is undone. All the work. Was my devotion not enough? Could not more mercy have been shown?"

His speech suddenly became more composed.

"Soon the demon invaders from space will be bearing down on us, and they will bring us death and destruction; hellfire and brimstone!" As he said this last line, I could see that he had raised his arms and pointed to the sky from where he cowered. I knew what he must be referring to.

Few men had considered the possibility of life on other planets, but just today, the news had broken that the most

8

compelling evidence of living organisms on another planet – Venus, of all things, with its hellish, inhospitable landscape – had been discovered.

He continued to wail on about this theme until it border-lined hysteria – hysterically lamenting mankind's situation – until I finally intervened. I found this line of thinking distasteful, and I quickly forged an annoyance at his selfish, defeatist despair.

"Pull yourself together! Man has faced all kinds of challenges – earthquakes, floods, wars – this isn't any different. Your religion is what is supposed to give you the faith you need to withstand the hardship."

The sobbing was replaced by a fractured, gasping breathing. I waited a minute for my response; my gut instinct reminding me of a potential threat. He spoke first.

"That sounds like something a demon would say."

I swallowed. The ante had been upped.

"I'm going to come out now, like you said."

I took a few steps back, anticipating his emergence. Although not a fighter I took up a fighting stance.

In the dying light, it took me a few seconds to focus to be able to make out any facial details on the shadow that now appeared no more than ten yards in front of me. He took several laboured steps towards me - in a manner not unlike sleepwalking.

He was of slight build and stood no more than 5 feet 8 tall – which put my mind to rest somewhat. He had a full head of fair hair, and his once flaxen curls had begun greying. The length had become wild and unkempt. He had large, round pale blue eyes which looked devoid of life. He had a scruffy, wispy beard that had no doubt been neglected and left to its own devices as his current crisis had developed. But this was not the disturbing part.

He came to a stop about five feet away from me, his arms hanging limply alongside him, still swaying. He was wearing a white t-shirt and jeans and as my focus sharpened in the hazy light, I could see his shirt had something splattered on it near the collar, and smeared marks wiped across the midriff. It was blood. The source of which seemed to be coming from his mouth, which was bloodied and hung open allowing the cool air to soothe the wound.

We stood there for a few moments opposite each other. Me staring at him. Him staring right through me.

"My God man, your mouth…. you need to get home and clean yourself up before you get an infection."

His mouth widened into a horrific, haunting smile. Blood now ran from the corners of his mouth. I suddenly longed for a jogger or a dog walker to stroll by.

"It doesn't matter this is Armageddon!" he laughed loudly, "ARMAGEDDON IS HERE!"

The laughter became raucous and noisy. As he laughed, he began running his fingers through his hair, smearing blood across his forehead. His head tipped backwards and as his mouth opened, for the first time I saw what had been causing this bloody mess.

"Who did that?"

I was ignored at first. I spoke again but louder, and in a more demanding fashion.

"Who did this? Stop laughing!"

The volume of his laughter gradually scaled back down, and his head levelled up until he met my eyeline again. He motioned as though about to take a sudden step forward, toying with me, before retreating - laughing to himself in a mocking fashion as I instinctively took a step back to maintain a safe distance.

"Did you know…." he began, "that in the early 1900's some Doctors believed that pulling out patients' teeth could cure them of madness?"

I swallowed hard. The realisation of why he was telling me this was grim beyond belief.

"No, I was not."

He nodded in acknowledgement – just a few times, slowly at first, but this soon descended into a feverish and wild shaking and thrashing about of his head in all directions. Then he froze still again.

"They believed that all metal disorders stemmed from disease and infection polluting the brain. They would extract the teeth, and if that didn't fix it, they would go even further. They would move on to the tonsils, adenoids and eventually their spleens, stomachs and colons too."

I was unqualified to respond, and instead, stood still – certain that his sermon would continue.

The man looked me dead in the eye and opened up his mouth. Once again, his pattern of movements of slow, calculated acts followed by frenzied fits continued.

He inserted his left hand into his mouth and used his thumb and forefingers to force and prop open the cavity. His right hand, with the speed of a lightning fast lightweight boxer reached up and began bashing and hitting his upper, first premolar. He hit it relentlessly, and when he got some purchase on it, he changed tact and frantically began jostling it in its jaw. I could hear a grinding sound manifest itself as the tooth loosened and became twisted in its socket as he ferociously wrestled with it.

"Stop, don't do that!" I pleaded.

I no longer think he could hear my words, as his focussed and savage attack on himself continued. All the while he emitted what can only be described as an audible growling noise. The final sound to be added to this sick symphony of suffering came next as I unmistakeably detected the sound of his periodontal ligament fibres at the root of his tooth being brutally torn from his jawbone.

Forsaking my own safety, I felt compelled to move towards him, but this time he violently shrugged in my direction, and backed off a few feet or so.

"NO."

I anxiously looked around, hoping that a passer-by would happen upon us. I muttered what amounted to no more than some incomprehensible protestations at his actions, which were ignored.

Glancing back at this man, I saw the final whip-crack motion of his wrist that removed the tooth from his head. He studied it for a second, before disgustedly casting it aside. Fresh blood must have been pouring from the wound, as for the next few seconds as he wiped his hands over his shirt, he repeatedly spat mouthfuls of blood on to the tarmac path on which he stood.

"I'm going to call you an ambulance," I stuttered, not totally convinced that was who I needed.

"NO," he shouted, "the Lord will deliver me from this evil yet. He will banish this disease from his flock, and it the non-believers will be driven asunder."

He reached back in his mouth once more and began fumbling around to identify another tooth to eradicate.

"STOP THIS!" I shouted, "this is madness."

I don't think he was even aware of my presence any longer, as he erupted into a stream of tongues. With no regard for the protocols of the pandemic, humanity dictated that I needed to subdue and restrain the man, before he did some irreparable harm to himself or somebody else.

I rushed the man, shoulder barging him as hard as I was able. It caught him off guard, and it briefly made him more lucid and present. I followed this up with a tackle at thigh height, throwing everything I had into the dive. I had not been any good at rugby in school, and had never mastered the rugby tackle, and as a result he did not go down to the ground exactly as I had envisioned.

Instead, he stumbled backwards, towards the direction of the culvert wall, and ended up tripping over his own feet, finishing up in a seated position on the grass with me clinging on loosely to his waist. He wailed like he was possessed and began flailing his arms around and kicking his legs. I brought my hands up to either side of my head to protect myself from his wild – and fortunately inaccurate and limp wristed – blows.

I rolled away from him, and he scrambled to his feet. As he sought to evade me and put some distance between us, he looked back at me, shouting, "DEMON!" as he did.

But darkness had arrived now, and he was not looking where he was going. I outstretched my arm in his direction and called out for him to come near to me, but I could not stop him in time.

He stumbled on the wall, and in the light of the moon I saw his body sweep over the wall almost in slow motion and disappear from view. The only reason I knew he hadn't vanished into a wormhole was because I heard the thud of his body after it fell through the air for 20 feet or so to base of the concrete floor below.

As I sat up on the grass, I froze completely still and tried to channel all of my energies into my sense of hearing, but I couldn't hear anything. No voices, no signs of movement. Terrified of what I might find, I got to my feet as silently as I possibly could. Partly so I could continue to listen for any signs of life, and partly out of a misguided early sense of guilt coupled with having no clear conviction on how I was going to handle all of the possible outcomes as yet.

I crept closer to the wall and peered slowly over. Not consciously aware that I had been holding my breath, I exhaled loudly as I looked down.

The curate's body lay beneath me, lifeless. The steady stream of water from the lake delicately washed over him as it exited down the large metal drain.

I was sure he was dead.

Dead directly as a result of his madness - manifested through his religious outbursts.

I prayed. I prayed that we have been divinely given the resources to deal with our present situation, or that it was all part of a greater plan we had not yet comprehended.

Or perhaps it was simply a vengeful act of a higher power, as depicted in the Old Testament.

"God help us," I whispered.

Car Pool

"Strike first, Strike Hard, No Mercy," I said as I just caught the fading green lumens of the Station Road traffic lights in time to sail through, condemning my successors to a short wait.

"What does that bullshit mean?" I could see Jennifer in my rear-view mirror, looking at me blankly.

Exasperated, I shook my head.

"Come on, you know. It's what Johnny says."

Jenn paused for a minute before slowly starting to nod, open mouthed.

"Ooohhhh, ok. I'm with you. Yes, I heard about that," she said, staring out the window at the closed shops that lined the village high street.

I rolled my eyes. How could she not have heard about it – everyone has been talking about it for at least the last month.

"Oh, have you," I answered in mocking tone of voice, keeping my eyes on the road whilst continuing to shake my head in a mild disbelief.

"Yes, I couldn't believe it when I heard." Then, as she munched her way through a mouthful of her Belvita morning biscuit from the packet on her lap, added, "Such a shame. I used to love him in Edward Scissorhands too."

This comment jarred me somewhat out of autopilot, and I quickly glanced back at her twice, frowning.

"Edward Scissorhands....?" I uttered before realisation dawned. "Not Johnny fucking Depp you wet lettuce."

Jenn looked at me with a bewildered face, silently pleading with me to share the answer with her.

"Go on then. Who is it?"

"Johnny? From Cobra Kai? The Netflix show? The best series ever!"

Jenn just kind of shrugged.

"1.4 billion minutes of this top quality programming was streamed and watched across just three days this summer. It's a global phenomenon!"

"Oh," she said as she went back to her Belvita. "I thought you meant the actor. He was in court accused of something like that."

"I don't think it would have taken that long to reach a verdict if they played a video of him saying that, would it!"

I glanced up into the rear view, chuckling to myself. Jenn was stifling a laugh too and sat there with a wide grin spread across her face that every couple of seconds would explode into a giggle. It was great to see her smiling again, and I didn't care that her mask had been pulled down to sit below her chin. With me in the driver's seat, and her in the rear seat to my left we were in excess of a metre anyway. Not like the old days though. She'd usually ride 'shotgun' with me on the way to work – and had done for nearly five years.

We went down the high street and took the left at the roundabout toward the dual carriageway. In ordinary

16

circumstances, we would leave half an hour earlier than we had done, but there was no need now. There was very little traffic around at the moment, and even when we did come across some, it moved along quickly and didn't delay us at all.

"Jenn, did I tell you about Saturday night?"

"No. What happened Saturday night?" she asked.

"I broke lockdown rules and went to a board game night at my mates house."

She looked fairly shocked and covered her mouth with her hand.

"Oh. That was naughty."

"Yeah – I felt a bit bad about it," I explained, "but I just love Risk."

"Oh, right. Well you need to be careful all the same."

I sighed, and chuckled, "No, it's a joke. I love Risk. The game Risk."

She thought about it for a second. Life slowly began returning to her eyes. There it is, there it is.

"Ooooohhh – Risk."

Ker-ching – the sound of the proverbial penny dropping. She laughed a little – not as much as the first time, but thankfully, it was there a little. Lockdown had hit her hard.

She had lived alone in a one bedroom flat the whole time I had known her, and she had never spoken about a boyfriend, or companion of any kind to me in that whole time. She was introverted in fact, but with people she was comfortable Jenn could be very witty and her humour very dry – notwithstanding some tendencies to be somewhat dim on occasion, which was often hilarious too.

I would call and message her now and again during the first enforced national lockdown and over time when I called, I could hear in her voice that any positive frame of mind she had maintained was deteriorating. After a few occasions – and a month or so in – she broke down in tears on the phone to me. She explained to me how, initially, the lockdown had actually made her feel calmer. The anxiety associated with having to go to work and sit in crowded offices whilst the increased threat of contracting a disease with no known vaccine, reduced.

When (almost) all of us were sent home, Jenn said it had meant that she no longer needed to constantly push herself outside of her comfort zone, and – furloughed from work, and safe at home in her flat – became more relaxed. The novelty of this wore off very soon after though, and she began to struggle with the lack of routine in her life and the sudden absence of all her social interactions. After a chance meeting in a Tesco Extra, I could see that her mood was alarmingly low, and so I took to speaking to her more frequently; just to check in with her.

It was during these calls that she opened up about how she used to suffer with panic attacks through her teenage years - way before the pandemic. Now she was beginning to experience a constant burden of worry about leaving the house due to the fear of contracting and/or spreading the virus – which in turn, left her highly anxious that these attacks would return. As time went on, a new concern arose - the fear of losing her job. And this played more and more on her mind, further making matters worse.

We had just begun settling into a routine again, having been called back to work in September – but now, the second wave had hit, and another lockdown had been mandated. And this time – having the benefit of hindsight and being familiar with the kind of uncertainty we would now face – it felt worse than the first in many ways.

We had been coasting down the dual carriageway when we reached the industrial estate where our office was based. As I turned into the side road, I slammed on the brakes.

"Bloody hell! Look at that!"

Jenn sprang into life, a little startled, "What is it?"

I slowed down and crawled to a stop at the side of the road and pointed to one of the units across the car park. Unit 6b once housed our favourite greasy spoon café – 'Kevin's Bacon'. For less than three quid you could pick up a crispy bacon roll containing at least 3 rashers of the crispiest, thickest, tastiest bacon and a cup of tea – all served up with Kev's trademark acerbic – and sometimes - X-rated humour and verbal repartee.

"Oh God," Jenn exclaimed with a level of panic equal to if I had just delivered a swift right hook to a small kitten in front of her. But the fear was real. "What the Christ is 'Vegan Food Club'?"

We both sat there dumbfounded for several seconds, just silently shaking our heads in self-pitying disbelief.

"Well that's it then. Another Corona casualty no doubt. Thank you very bloody much 2020!"

I briefly considered punctuating this by bringing my fist down on my dashboard in faux outrage - but didn't. It was still enough for Jenn to let out a little laugh before covering her mouth.

I pulled up the handbrake and turned around and said – only half joking, "I'm sorry Jennifer. But I do not see anything to be laughing about at this time."

"I'm sorry," she continued to chuckle, "It's just the slogan underneath."

I turned back around and read it out loud.

"First rule of Vegan Food Club. Tell Everyone about Vegan Food Club!" Personally, I couldn't bring myself to laugh, although had to admit it was quite witty.

"That's about bloody right anyway."

I let off the handbrake, still shaking my head, and we continued our drive just a few more blocks along to our building, which was the last one on the right. I never had a problem parking the car. Behind the factory was a housing estate, and most of the factory line operatives lived on this estate. Years ago, someone had even cut a hole in the rear perimeter chain link fence – meaning they could just skip through it, ending up in the rear car park. Suited me as it normally meant that I had my choice of spaces. Today though – and since the start of this period of enforced closure - the car park had a long chain drawn across the entrance preventing me from entering the grounds at all, other than on foot. Even if I had been able to access the site, all of the companies' currently unrequired delivery vans dominated the parking area.

I pulled up on the pavement at the front – taking care to ensure that I wasn't encroaching on to the bus stop space, marked out in thick yellow paint, that lay just behind me. Across the road was my favourite restaurant – The Harvester – and when it had opened during August, me and Jenn had treated ourselves on three different occasions to a meal, after work, over there. Greedily snatching as much of our 50% contribution from the Government as we could afford.

We sat there quietly for a few minutes in the shadow of the dour, grey, two storey building, that was built sometime in the 70's. It was probably never an architectural revelation even at that time, but I would imagine that when it was new, it looked okay. I could see cigarette butts strewn around the car park, and the A4 note that Jenn had hastily written in marker pen back in March, had been recycled for this second lockdown, and stuck to the door (this time with gaffer tape) seconds before it was locked shut for at least another month.

"CLOSED DUE TO VIRUS".

We had all felt a sense of dread that if the company was forced into a second lockdown, then that could be it.

Manufacturing could have continued, but our place hadn't. That was the most obvious sign. If the management had just kept on a skeleton staff to keep things moving; to keep the cashflow going, I would feel more optimistic. But they didn't. They furloughed everyone – at every level of the business – the minute the scheme was announced, and that was it. Thank God the scheme was extended until March next year. I only hope that it's enough to give them some breathing room.

It wasn't just COVID, we were spiralling downhill years leading up to this. Manufacturing in general is tough in the UK, and to the management teams' credit, they had done an incredible job weathering the storm to get this far. Myself, and most of my colleagues, feared that this would be the final nail in their coffin. They can't keep continually swimming upstream. The unit production costs of washing lines are considerably cheaper in other parts of the world. China pressed us hard – gradually destroying our ability to remain profitable.

We sat in silence for a few minutes, until I turned around and smiled weakly.

"Shall we listen to some music on the way home?"

I saw a tear run down Jenn's face, and she nodded, wiping the tear away with the back of her hand. I turned on the only radio station that was permitted in my car – Planet Rock – and allowed Lynyrd Skynyrd to temporarily transport me away from our reality of 70's industrial estates and the sound of my squeaking fanbelt, and into the fantasy of me cruising up a hot, desert highway in a pink Cadillac for the whole 9 minutes and 8 seconds (it was the full version) of 'Freebird'.

We didn't say much until we pulled back up outside Jenn's place a short time later.

Jenn looked at me. More focussed than she had looked all morning. "Thank you…. I know it's ridiculous, I just want you to know it how much it helps."

I smiled back at her, "Trust me. It's my favourite bit of the day too."

She smiled back.

"Maccy D's breaky on the way tomorrow?"

Jenn nodded enthusiastically and got out the car. Slamming the door too hard as bloody usual. I lowered the passenger front window.

"Oi!" I yelled after her. She spun around. "You'll have to be finding someone else to carpool with if you slam that bloody door again."

She paused for a second, then flicked up both middle fingers before turning and walking off. I could see her laughing to herself as she continued up the path to her building.

Mission accomplished for another day.

Unsanitary

"Ok, ok come in, but I need you to hurry the fuck up."
I couldn't be bothered arguing anymore, especially as we were getting nowhere. As per, they hardly spoke a word of English and I had places to be. It was fucking typical of Ronnie to do this to me. He knew I had somewhere to be tonight.

There was four of them – all big, burly fellas - and they all lumbered in carrying their machines and equipment. The biggest one of the lot was even dragging a large suitcase behind him.

"What's in there then? Staying over the night are yu'?" I asked him, sarcastically.

They all wore full Hazmat type suits with the hoods drawn up over their heads and, of course, face masks (the white, vented kind that spray painters use) which fully covered their mouths and confined most of their beards to within it. This meant I could only see their eyes – and even then, two of them wore glasses. It was bloody hard to tell, but I don't think any of them smiled or laughed at my quip. Fuck it anyway, let them get in, get the job done and get out.

They moved through the little entrance corridor from the back door and walked the 30 feet or so into the main showroom. 'Diamond Rons' had been going since Ronnie set it up almost 25 years ago. Jewellery and watches were his thing. Did a fair bit of pawn broking recently – nothing too hot, but likewise, he didn't ask too many questions either. It was a decent size shop, just under 1000 square foot. The High Street had gone to the dogs the last few years – like everywhere else – but we had enough wheeling and dealing smarts to keep ticking over.

We specialised in the pieces up to about a grand. Few bits and bobs over – had a few Rolex watches probably worth five or six grand each that we'd bought – but in the main our custom either came from middle class blokes getting their wives a birthday or anniversary present, or young couples picking out engagement rings. We normally reeled them in by offering a bit of a deal to close the sale.

Business this year had been quite good – and I had done very well. When we had to shut the doors, me and Ron ran it off social media, local free ad groups and we done both a click and collect, and a local drop off service. Technically, Ronnie had furloughed me, but he'd pay me some commission in cash on any sales I would make this way – so I was coining it in working from home mainly. We'd just been getting back into it the groove and fuck me we had to close again. Still, we were back open in time for Christmas. It would've 'urt to miss that.

I had just finished locking the place up. I'd cashed the till up, locked the front door and closed the steel shutters on the shop windows – and it was then that my guests had rocked up, just as I was about to leave.

"So how long are you lot going to need here then?" I asked as they began opening their bags and getting their equipment out.

They moved in a hypnotic, robotic manner and – without looking up – the first bloke I'd spoken to grunted in a deep Eastern European accent, "We will be approximately one half hour."

Half an hour. Bollocks. I had to be at the Embassy Lounge by then or I'd miss my time slot.

"Come on, lads, it's only a small shop I reckon you won't need more than twenty minutes?"

The main guy paused, looked back at me, and simply shook his head. I left it there. He seemed more personable when he turned up at the door, but there was something about his vibe now that made me not want to challenge this. I just nodded back at him as he removed a curious looking device from his bag that looked like a cross between an internet router and a birthday cake - densely packed with black rubber candles.

This was going to fuck everything up. Ronnie had left at midday today and didn't mention this to me at all. I was doing the late shift tonight - though I always slipped off by 6.30 – and Margaret was opening up in the morning. Sorted, until these geezers turned up.

Margaret was fucking useless. Should have retired years ago. Ron must have only kept her on out of loyalty. She turned up and left like clockwork but everything that she did in between was dogshit. She was slow, she had no hustle.... I've heard her talk customers out of items that she thought was too expensive for them or tell customers that the stuff they were trying on didn't suit them. What's up with that?

Of course it fucking suits them if they are going to give you money for it that you will then get a cut of. And her singing. Always bloody singing. Trust me, if you have been out on a rager the night before and are coming down faster than a fat kid on a see-saw, her fucking singing would make your soul weep.

I noticed one of the guys standing up and came towards me. He motioned toward the door that separated the corridor and the showroom.

"Now we close. You stay out here. Ozone gas we use – dangerous."

Once he'd finished saying the last word, he gestured with his hands like the conductor of an orchestra, to communicate gases rising in the air. As he did, he also inhaled deeply from beneath the mask – his barrel chest filling out even further, looking ever more imposing. Again, I meekly nodded, and he closed the door. The bright light of the showroom dwindled until I was left in the dark hallway. The only light coming from an unsheathed economy bayonet lightbulb swinging freely in the kitchen.

The half an hour I would have to wait was underway.

.
.
.

Oh, fuck this! I wonder if Margaret is around to help me out. I could normally win her over with a bit of my trademark cheeky charm. I could tell her how much I loved her singing. Or her 'Bread and Butter pudding' that she would bring in almost weekly. Fuck me, I'd rather lick the worn-out slot of a cash machine. At least that way I might get lucky with some traces of cocaine! Anything - other than have a slice of that. The only time during this pandemic

I wish that I had lost my fucking sense of taste was when she brought that little delight in.

I couldn't keep Sofia waiting. I'd hustled hard to get her to have a drink with me and I'd taken a few risks to keep some things from her. Didn't want to balls it up now. I was close. I only wanted to fuck her once.

I went back towards our little kitchen area where my phone lay on the table. I'll give Margaret a try. She could be here in ten minutes.

I caught sight of myself in the mirror and rehearsed the call in my head, trying to sound as genuine as possible.

'Margaret. How are you? Yes, it's Jay. I'm okay my love, I'm okay. Did you have something nice for your supper? Oh – I hope you left me some you little devil...ha...ha...anyway you know how you are like my second Mum. How do you fancy saving my bacon tonight? I will work back a shift for you – for free......wait.....you will? YOU are a life saver.' I had no intention of doing her shift for free of course, and I knew she would be too polite to take me up on it.

Something along those lines would do. I picked up my phone and rang her number.

Nothing happened. It just went back to the menu screen.

Looking carefully at the screen this time, I pressed her name firmly to make the call, and the screen changed to the 'dialling' screen. Within two seconds there was a beep – indicating it was terminating the attempt – and once again, it returned me to the home screen.

"What the fuck is happening here? I haven't missed my bill."

Trying a couple more times – even with one of the attempts seeing me waving the phone around in the air – reaped the same results. Looking at my phone closely, I could see that I had no signal. That was unusual. In fact, I can't ever remember having a problem with the signal in the shop.

Shit. Time was ticking.

The only other phone we had was in the showroom, by the till. They'd only closed the door less than a minute ago, I'm sure it'd be alright if I quickly went in to use it.

I darted up the hall to the door leading into the showroom. I rapped twice on the door, shouted out loud "Just need to come in a minute," and began to open it.

It had barely opened a crack, when I felt the door coming back against me with the unexpected force of a charging shoulder. The power slammed the door shut loudly into its frame and I lost my footing, going over like a felled skittle.

From within, one of them shouted, "We tell you. No come in please!"

"Fucking hell, alright. Did you have to do that? What are you spraying around in there? Agent Orange?"

There was no reply, just the low hum of something that sounded like a vacuum cleaner.

As I sat up, I winced in pain when I inhaled deeply and tensed up my stomach muscles. I must have bruised my ribs. Bollocks. I gingerly got to my feet and flinched again as I coughed a few times and triggered off the pain. I needed a sit down for a minute.

I held my hand across my stomach and pressed in on the ribs on the opposite site; hunched myself slightly over and walked delicately walked toward to kitchen. What a wanker. Way too heavy handed. I'll ask Ron in the morning the name of the company, ring them up and give them some shit for that.

I sat down on a stool in the kitchen to think. I tried making a few more calls to Margaret on my mobile phone, but the same thing happened. No signal. That meant I couldn't ring – or message – Sofia too to tell her I'd been held up. Shit!

It had been hard enough as it was arranging this. To be honest, I felt a bit bad about the whole thing. It hadn't been long since me and the Mrs had gotten back together. We had decided to give it another shot for about eight months ago, after our little trial separation.

I found myself going over it again in my head.

It had started off with me storming out of the house after she was constantly giving me shit for having too many nights out on the lash. I told her, it's my hobby! I got loads of mates who (normally) play football twice a week or spend every evening at the gym. I'm not interested in any of that, I just love relaxing and having a beer with some of my mates a few times a week. What makes that any different? She didn't use to like the fact that I would have a bit of a dabble with some recreational drugs either - always going on about that too. Doing my head in. I used to say to her – 'my problem is that I'm too honest with you'. I should have just lied and told her that I was fucking off out for a game of badminton instead.

Me and Jess had been together for ten years and had two kids. Two little boys – 5 and 8. Little diamonds those lads, love 'em to bits. I was gonna miss them but, I told her, it's for their own good that I get out of here. They don't want to listen to us arguing and fighting all the time. It's not fair.

She cried the house down, and begged me to stay, but the time wasn't right. Plus, my head had gone.

I went back to my Mother's house – it was only 100 yards round the corner. Slept back in my old bedroom. Well, I did on the nights I made it back home anyway – ha ha. I always sent a little bit of money up to her, you know, what I could afford. But I stayed out of the way so we could all have a breather. I did see the kids that year once or twice from memory. I definitely saw Jack twice anyway because my Mother brought them both over one afternoon for tea and a visit and I went to the hospital to see Jack when he fell off the kerb in the street and had to have 12 stitches in his chin. The car park prices are fucking extortionate there. I made sure I didn't stay more than 30 minutes. They're not mugging me off.

I got into a bit of a routine most days. Drag myself up from bed. Shower. Get out for work at Ronnie's. Finish 5.30 or 6.30, depending. Straight to the 'Coach and Horses' on the corner for a couple there and a game of pool. From there, quite often it was into town. A few more pubs. Sometimes a bit a livener. Kebab and home. There was a group of four of us. I was there almost every day, and it was normally at least one, sometimes two, of the others keeping me company. It was only a few times that I ended up going on my own.

I had a crack on that Tinder. That was a right laugh. Youngsters have it easy these days. When I first started going to pubs and clubs, you had to work for it. I mean *really* fucking work for it. Dance your way over, catch their eye, few drinks, bit of conversation and even then it could be hit or miss. Nowadays, you go on the app, look through a load of pictures and just swipe on the one you fancy, and get straight down to business with what you're after. Took out a right few girls off that. Some lovely ones - some monsters. But it doesn't matter, it was only for a bit of sport.

After that year, I bumped into Jess at the Coach when I was there after work one day – just before I started working from home. She was all dolled up to go into town to meet her mate. Looked lovely to be fair. Short leopard print skirt and hair in pig tails. Well, she never made it into town that night let me tell you. We stayed at the Coach for a few more drinks, then straight back round to our house. The boys must have recognised my voice because they came running into the bedroom. It wasn't exactly good timing though, and I had to tell them to piss off because Daddy was a 'bit busy' and that I'd give them a cuddle in the morning.

It felt like finding your favourite old pair of jeans you thought you'd chucked out, and slipping them back on, and before we knew it, everything just went back to normal really. I brought back my suitcase of clothes the next day and we carried on without missing a beat. It was pretty good again at first. She tried to stop giving me a hard time and I said I'd try to not have so many nights out. It was easy to stick too at first since Boris shut all the pubs for months. But when they opened them all back up, you couldn't keep me away. I'd missed them badly. It's who I am. Ronnie knows me better than I know myself, and he calls me 'The Bon Vivant of Becks Hill'. He told me it's someone who devotes themselves to socialising. I like that; I make him right.

After eight months back together – and most of it cooped up together in a 2 bedroom terrace - I'm struggling. Don't get me wrong, it's nice being able to see the boys almost every day, but I have started telling some porky pies about where I've been or where I'm going. I just don't think I was made for 100% commitment. It doesn't suit me. I've seen documentaries – on BBC1 mind you, proper shows – about people like me. People who have so much to give they can't be exclusively with one person. What I'm doing is normal in the animal kingdom you know. Understanding this helped me combat any pangs of guilt or shame that I sometimes got from time to time.

The way I see it is that it's not different to one of my mates spending two hours down the gym and sauna. They go in, do their thing, it relaxes them, and they come out feeling better in themselves. I go out, have a few drinks, sometimes I end up having a laugh with a bird, and I come home. I'm better for it so everyone benefits. My boys. Jess. It's got to be good for my mental health too. Course, I know she won't see it like that. None of them do. So, it's just easier to keep it quiet, and I can keep doing my thing. Hurting no one really, is it?

Same as with the drugs. I had more cash than I'd ever had before. I literally couldn't spend it this year and staying in every day had saved me a fortune. When I could go out, I treated myself a bit. Bought a bit more than I would had done before. I know what I'm doing though, know my limits. I had a little bag on me tonight. I had enough for Sofia too - if she wanted any – but mainly it was to make sure I had the right energy levels after a long day at work.

In fact, I think I might do a little line now.....

Fucks sake – how long have they been already? Probably only ten minutes. I need to use that phone.

I marched back toward the showroom door – this time thumping hard on it with the side of my fist, keen to not repeat the mistake I made the last time I tried to gain access. A few moments passed, and I heard the vacuum cleaner noise stop, and footsteps.

The door opened enough for me to be able to see one of the guys' head in the gap.

"Hello?" he said.

"Mate I need to use the phone in there – can you just give me one minute?"

The man sternly shook his head, making a chirping/tutting noise from between his lips.

"No entry to room. The gas make you sick."

Before I could protest, one of his colleagues called him from behind (sounded like he called him 'Nay' – or it could just be Romanian for 'Oi') and he indicated to me he would be one moment with his index finger and closed the door.

When the door re-opened a few seconds later, the man was holding a pen and piece of paper, which he thrust at me. When I had collected them off him, he used his right hand to squiggle in thin air which I took as him wanting me to sign the piece of paper. I didn't even look at it. Keen to get things moving as swiftly as possible, I signed on a dotted line at the bottom, and handed them both back to him.

"Multumesc," he said before disappearing back inside and shutting the door behind him.

I would just have to wait, and hope that Sofia would still be waiting when I got there. I was going to get an Uber, but I'll just drive my car down and leave it in town instead. That will save me five minutes. It'll be okay. Look on the bright side – if she waits, then I'm definitely in.

Sofia was bloody gorgeous. A right Eastern European beauty with jet black hair and those piercing, entrancing blue eyes. Intelligent, yet somehow rebellious.

She had come into the shop a few weeks looking at some jewellery. We didn't have anything she wanted – sounded like she had a serious budget in mind to blow, and we didn't have anything that upmarket to show her. I didn't get out of her what either her or her husband did, but it was clear she had a right few quid at her disposal.

And look, I'm no mug. Whilst it's not like I'm so ugly I make blind kids cry, I know that I am punching well above my weight with this one – but what can I say? We got on. We had a laugh and a bit of a chat. The old trademark charm wins the day again! I searched and added her on Facebook – wasn't too hard to find a Sofia Lupulescu based near me – and messaged back and forth, building to a meet.

Course, I acquainted myself with her photo library – particularly the bikini ones from her holiday to the Maldives last year. Very nice. Liking a few of these must've got across my devilish intentions, and tonight was going to be the night.

Was.

Fucking hell! They're going to blow it for me. I'm not having this anymore.

With a rush of blood, I marched up to the showroom door again, smashed it five times with the side of my fist again and shouted in.

"Sorry lads – got to go now. Been called away for an emergency with my kids. If not finished, I write down number of woman who works here – lives down the road – you finish, lock shop with key and take to her…"

35

The door flew open, I heard the loud crack as his fist smashed me across the mouth, and then everything went black. I must have been asleep before I even hit the floor.

I slowly opened my eyes and lay motionless on the floor trying to assess where I was and why I was there. I could smell a strong, sickly sweet smell. Like the smell of a hospital.

I was enveloped in darkness.

With vague recollections of being cuffed, I silently and deliberately felt around where my body lay. Felt like worn-out, old carpet tiles. I removed a handkerchief that was laying on my face, sat up and leaned on my elbows. As I opened my mouth and moistened my arid lips, I tasted the metallic bitter taste of dried blood - which had turned sticky. I soon realised that that my nose and mouth area were coated in it.

As my eyes adjusted to the shadows, I could make out large boxes around most of the rooms' perimeter – although they looked out of focus.

I attempted to get to my feet without making a sound. I winced in pain when I inadvertently moved my jaw, and when I used my hands to push myself up on the floor, they felt bruised and sore. I got on to the soles of my feet, although still in a prone position, and using every ounce of strength in my thighs raised my body up into a standing position so slowly as for the movement to be undetectable.

Still in darkness, I was bracing myself for either another thump, or some kind of other assault – but none came. I stood perfectly still – holding my breath – and just allowed my eyeballs to flicker up, down, left, and right to try and establish my surroundings.

I was sure that I was in the middle of the showroom floor, but it was the sound of the Grandfather clock we had in the corner that had confirmed it to me beyond doubt. In the silence of the night, and the empty shop, I could hear it clearer than ever before. The ticking heartbeat being driven on by the omnipresent clicking noise of the mechanical gears as they slid against each other. Ron had turned off the chime, so it hadn't celebrated the passing of an hour for years.

Growing more confident that I was alone, I gently moved my head around to increase my circle of vision. I couldn't really see anything. Just shadows, and the large box shape items around the perimeter of the room, which I deduced must be the jewellery counters we worked from behind.

I stepped back to look behind me, and gingerly took my first steps towards sound of the ticking. I became aware that I had instinctively begun to hold my arms out to the side like a tightrope walker, but with my elbows bent and palms outstretched. When I got to the clock, I'd be able to turn the light on and see where we are. I could also get that Leatherman tool that Ron kept under the till. One of those little multi-tool type, penknife affairs. The blades on them were only small but fuck me they were sharp. It could go right through your finger as easily as a tomato. That would be a leveller if anyone was still here. I'm no stranger to a tear up, but come on, I can't go toe to toe with four of them.

I started to wind myself up that they were lying in wait for me for somewhere in the building, so my slow controlled walk to the clock became large clumsy strides where I almost slipped on a wet spot on the carpet.

When I reached it, I fumbled around on the wall next to it, looking for the light switch. I found it, and clicked it back and forth a few times, but nothing. They probably smashed the bulbs. What was going on? I felt my heartbeat grow more rapidly and heavily through my chest as I pondered over the confusion of what was happening.

I felt along the counter until I reached the door to the back area. I took a deep breath and began to lower the handle as slowly and quietly as I could manage. I kept my body low to the ground and peered down the hall once I had enough of a view. I could see a clear path to the rear exit. So long as the kitchen was clear, I would lock the rear door and go get the torch from the cleaning cupboard to have a look around. What was the time too? I was sure my date is fucked now – might as well forget about meeting Sofia tonight. Have to make up something proper elaborate to get around her.

With the door wide open, I crept down the hall and peeped around the door frame and into the kitchen. There was no one there. A blind panic rushed over me, and I seized my coat from the back of the door, scrambled around in the pockets for the keys and ran to the rear exit to lock and secure it. I put both bolts across and leaned against the wall, panting and perspiring – my heart feeling as though it was going to burst out through my chest. I wished I'd left the gear alone earlier now.

My phone still lay on the kitchen table, and although I only had 6% battery life left, I turned the torch on intending to use it to guide me to the cleaning cupboard. I noticed on the screen that it was just before 8.30pm. Strangely, after my earlier lack of phone reception, I now had 27 missed calls. Couple from Sofia (saved under Bazza, for obvious reasons), several from my Mrs - but most were from Ron.

I grabbed the torch, and after hitting it with the butt of my palm a few times, it blinked on although the light it gave out was dim, with a pissy-yellow hue to it. It would do for a minute – my phone was about to die on me.

I headed back to the showroom with it. It must have been a robbery. I couldn't have pissed them off that much by asking them to hurry up, could I? Well, I did ask a few times. My jaw is a bit sore where I was clocked, and my nose must be busted up what with all the blood, but to be honest, I've had worse tunings. Maybe they just thought they'd teach me a lesson and leave me there sparked out. I opened the door and went in.

The torchlight showed that they had packed all their gear up and taken it with them. The place had been left tidy. All the glass counters were intact, and there was no sign of broken glass on the floor. I scanned the contents, and at a glance, all the jewellery seemed to be in their places. As I did, I could even see that the lightbulbs from the ceiling lights had indeed been taken out, and carefully placed on top of one of the glass counters.

Oh well, that sorts it then. They just thought that I was a chopsy prick and gave me a clip, by the look of things. What kind of company employs people who do that though? I'll have a word with Ron tomorrow and find out who they are. Bastards.

Ah well. Let's call it a night. I'll put that bulb back in and might as well chip off home and watch the football instead.

I walked to the centre of the room and found the wet patch on the carpet again - almost slipping in the process for the second time. Reaching up on my tip-toes, I twisted the light bulb back into its socket, and the light flashed, blinding me at first.

I batted my eyelids over and over, trying to clear the lights in front of my eyes. And through the blinking, like a Zoetrope animation device sitting on top of a record player at 45 rpm I saw her. I thought it was an illusion. I rubbed my eyes which just made my vision even more hazy, but nonetheless left me in no doubt about what I was seeing.

Sofia's body lay slumped against the side of the display cabinets that housed the engagement rings. The one thing keeping her body from dropping to the ground was the fact that the top of her skull, from her repeatedly bashed in head had hooked itself on to the corner of the display cabinet.

I heard the torch hit the ground, and the battery compartment cracking off when it exploded on to the floor. No. What is this?

In a daze, I approached her lifeless body – dressed in the splendour of a red cocktail dress. I could barely manage to put one foot in front of the other. My legs felt as though they had no bones running through them anymore and they trembled relentlessly. I stamped my way over to her, sobbing. Wiping my running nose, I realised that the blood all over me was not coming from my nose - and didn't even appear to be my blood either.

Panting heavily, I put my hands on her shoulders to turn her around and gently lay her down. She would not move. The blows had been so violent and relentless, the corner of the cabinet was now deeply embedded in her skull. Her body trailed like a coat that had been hung on to the peg of a coat stand.

'No, no, this can't be.'

I raised my leg and used all my might to prise her head up and off the cabinet. There was a loud slurping noise, as it sharply came free – sending me reeling backwards and slipping on the wet patch. I ended up on my back on the floor – with the corpse of Sofia on top of me. What was left of her face, just an inch from mine.

Her porcelain skin was blotchy and cold. Her perfect smile had become a graveyard of tombstone teeth, where impact after impact had knocked most of them out of place, or simply removed them altogether. Her left temple and upper check bone had been decimated – with bones having been shattered into small fragments from the blows that lay sprinkled around the large cavity that had been bored and hollowed out. And her once striking eyes were now bloodshot and white, where the pupils had rolled back into her head – or that was how her left one looked.

Her right eye had a pen – the very pen I was asked to use earlier to sign a document – stabbed directly into the centre of it.

I screamed – a long, wailing scream. Either no noise was coming out, or I was deaf to it. I wriggled and tried to get out from underneath her, but I couldn't think straight and summon the strength. Alive and complete she weighed no more than 9 stone, but I was sapped. Between sobs, I continued to try to push her away. I pushed at her head, and her neck arched back and revealed red hand marks all over it.

Gripping her hair with my left hand, and holding her head away from me, I outstretched my aching, bruised right hand, and looked at the palm. I lined it up perfectly against the marks on her throat.

A match.

The fear summoned a burst of inhuman strength in me, and I was able to get the leverage to push her alongside me on the floor. I tried to regulate my breathing.

'Ok, fucking breath, fucking breath. Think Jay, think.'

My head was spinning. I felt as though I had unbridled energy, but at the same time felt comatose and unable to move. It was like an out of body experience.

My phone vibrated and made a piercing beep to indicate that the battery was about to die, and the phone would close down in just 30 seconds. It allowed me time to manage one more viewing of the screen, and I saw that there was a text message from Ron.

"Just stay where you are, we are on our way to help now. Everything will be okay."

What the fuck? How does he…...?

With the last 20 seconds of phone life, I scrolled up to see what that was in response to.

At 7.45pm, I sent Ron a message. It read:

"Ron, please come to the shop. I've really fucking done it this time. I think she's dead. Help me Ron."

The screen went black as I heard two vehicles, speeding down the street towards the shop. The sound of their blaring sirens increasing, until it became deafening as they screeched to a halt outside.

The Corona Clause

This was always going to be a tough conversation. Maisie was smart young lady. Her reading and math were at a level significantly above the rest of her class, and she had boundless enthusiasm. I had anticipated some curiosity on the subject but had also hoped that her Mum would have been cornered on this one before she got me. Typically, it had been on the night I had taken her up to clean her teeth and put her nightie on.

She had first mentioned it in between toothpaste spits into the sink. Half gargling, half talking – still with plenty of foamy toothpaste stored in her cheeks – she had asked me:

"So how is Santa going to deliver my presents this year?"

She was only 8, but I had set myself the expectation that she would believe for at least two more Christmases. I wasn't ready to let it go yet.

"What do you mean?" I gingerly enquired – simply to buy time, as I knew exactly what she meant.

"With the coronavirus? How can he travel around the world?" she went on, with the toothpaste gurgling around in her mouth.

I have to admit, I let myself down somewhat here. I just didn't think my reply through enough.

I had reached the end of a busy day where I had been in work for 12 hours. I had made the dinner, cleaned up, put on a wash and now I was mainly focussing on the glass of wine I was going to pour when Maisie had been put to bed. I was so close to the finish line for the day that, without thinking, I brusquely – and cheaply – said:

"Well he's magic honey. He can do anything."

Well, if I did.

Unsatisfied with this hasty attempt to swiftly resolve the discussion, she looked at me with complete exasperation at my condescending, and ill-advised comment.

"Dad. There are things he will need to consider this year. Extra things."

As she spoke, some of the toothpaste she was fighting to keep in began escaping from the side of her mouth. I seized the opportunity to buy some time.

"You finish brushing your teeth nicely a minute, and we'll talk about it when you are tucked up in bed."

I went in her room to close her blinds, turn her duvet down, and to think of how I was going to tackle this – in a logical and practical fashion. Within a matter of minutes, I could hear her running the tap for the last time, the 'chinking' noise of her toothbrush being returned to the china toothbrush holder and the sound of the towel hitting the floor as she used it and then put it back on the towel rail properly.

She trotted back into the room – a collage of all the Disney princesses on her nightie – and hopped into her bed, pulling the duvet up underneath her armpits. And looked at me.

"So how is he going to be able to fly around the world?"

This got us off to what I thought was a straightforward start. He didn't go around on easyJet after all.

"Well, he uses his sled and his reindeers to get around - so he doesn't have to worry about any flying restrictions."

She nodded throughout and waited for me to stop talking so she could go on.

"Yes, but isn't the point of it to stop the spread of coronavirus around the world. So even if he flies himself into the countries, won't all the different countries want to stop him?"

"Well, I would think they make an exception for Santa. They would all want their children to be visited by him after all, so I can't imagine that any of them would want to stop him from coming."

"But isn't that irresponsible though, Daddy? Won't Santa think to himself that it is not a good idea to go to every single different country on Earth and will decide to not do Christmas this year?"

"Santa won't take any risks that will hurt anybody. He will definitely have to be extra careful this year – you're right. But he will make sure that he visits every child - safely."

"Will he wear gloves when he goes into every child's house?"

I smiled. It wasn't too tough after all.

"Yes honey, he will."

Then the ante was raised a little.

"But will he replace them every single time?"

"What do you mean?"

"Well my teacher said that it is worse to wear the same gloves than to just wash your hands thoroughly every time

45

after you touch something, because the gloves hold more germs."

"Uh – yes I suppose he will. He won't be able to wash his hands in every house he visits in case he wakes the family up."

"So how many pairs of gloves will he use?"

Without contemplating it for too long, I plucked a figure out of the air.

"Ooh – let me see…uh..maybe…a hundred million."

Maisie wrinkled up her nose (so cute) and laughed. "A hundred million! Daddy!"

I could sense that I was being pushed out on to a limb here.

"What?" I asked with feigned surprise. I knew what I was about to be picked up on.

"There's more children than that in the world."

"Oh – ok, well that was just a guess. Go on then smart guy – how many are there?"

"My teacher told us there's like 2 billion children in the world, so even if lots have brothers and sisters, that's still way more than one hundred million isn't it?"

Before I could answer this question, she shot me a serious look and hit me with another question.

"He doesn't miss anyone out now, does he?"

I was grateful to have avoided another potential pitfall, as 'not all kids get a visit from Santa' was one of the multiple choice answers my brain had presented to me. Maisie had given me a bit of 'phone a friend' type assistance by asking this loaded question.

"Gosh no. Of course he doesn't."

"So how many pairs of gloves will he need?"

I harrumphed around with my hands out to the side, palms up, for a few seconds before blurting out, "I don't know... I suppose about a billion."

She scrunched up her little nose and shrieked out loud with laughter.

"A billion pairs of gloves! So, he will change the gloves on each of his hands two billion times in a night?"

"Uh – yes. I suppose he will."

"Where will he get a billion pairs of gloves from?"

I was starting to feel quite belittled and began longing more and more for my wine.

"I don't know. I guess his factory halted production on the toys and started making them earlier in the year."

"Oh."

She paused her interrogation and considered this for a moment. I took this as an opportunity to leave, but as I leaned in to kiss her forehead goodnight, the line of questioning was reopened.

"So, did he ever have a lockdown in the North Pole?"

Easy one.

"No, he carried on. There wasn't a single case of it reported in the North Pole," I confidently presumed.

"So do his elves have to socially distance when they work in the factory?"

"Um – I think so. It was probably done as a precaution. Just to make sure."

"So, did he have to sack any of his workers?"

"Sack any of them? What do you mean?"

"Well if not as many people can work in the factory anymore, then where can they go?"

I needed to pull something out of the bag here. I needed to divulge some kind of revelation to her. I think I had something.

"Well – you're old enough now. I think I can tell you."

Maisie sat up now and moved the pillows to behind her back, listening intently.

"You know how you like to go through the toy catalogues and pick out what you want for Christmas?"

She nodded enthusiastically.

"Well, Santa and his team of elves don't actually build them in his workshop from this year on. Many of the elves who couldn't work in the factory anymore - because of social distancing - were taken into a different building and Santa made them into his digital team. So now, me and your Mum put an order in to his digital team, and they actually source the presents from the shops."

She squinted a little and nodded in some small degree of satisfaction at this explanation.

'*Come on. Come back from that one then,*' I thought to myself – actually tasting the Rioja.

"So, did he build a new workshop for them?"

"Yes – I believe he re-purposed some of the workshop as they weren't making as many toys and didn't need all the space anymore. And then he built an extension on to it."

"So, do Amazon deliver to the North Pole then?"

Well played.

"I have no doubt that they do."

"How will he meet all the children this year so they can tell him what they want?"

"I ….don't think he has announced that yet. Maybe he will do Zoom meetings with children."

"I don't mind not meeting him. I've met him lots of times now. Three times last year," she proudly announced.

She's not bloody wrong either. It used to be an occasion to take your kids to see Santa in his grotto just before Christmas every now. Nowadays, in December, the hairy bastard is everywhere you turn. I tried to keep it sacred and special by booking some decent events where they get to meet him – for example, these big 'Winter Wonderland' type events, or a special Christmas lunch at a nearby hotel. But this gets watered down somewhat when the day before your big annual event arrives, and you find out that it's actually the third time this week your kid has seen him.

In addition to the trip to the nearby garden centre to see him, he turned up at a school assembly and then - that very same night - was seen being pulled around the estate on a small wooden sled built on to a trailer, by a twenty-five-year-old Land Rover Discovery with heavily rusted wheel arches. If that didn't make it unconvincing enough, then on top of that, he was also rattling a collection tin as he went (collecting money to support the local amateur dramatics club!), handing out fun size packs of Rolos and wishing everyone a 'Merry Christmas' in a thick Welsh accent from beneath his one dimensional fabric beard.

When I first bought a re-usable face mask – the cheap type where two pieces of fabric have been cut from the same template, and crudely stitched together down the middle – it brought to mind this shit beard he had worn that day. This type of Santa onslaught already eroded the magic somewhat without throwing old Discovery's and shit beards into the mix.

"OK – time for sleep no…"

I was interrupted again. This was not good; I now needed the wine.

"But how old is he again, Dad?"

"Uh..," I treaded carefully on this one. I could see where she was going, so I…

"I know he is very, very old!"

Bollocks – interrupted again. Must think faster.

"If he is very, very old, doesn't that mean he has to stay at home and not go anywhere because it would be very dangerous if he caught Corona?"

"Well…I guess it's all relative. For an average man, being a hundred years old – or even a thousand years old – would mean you were very old. But if you lived for ten thousand years then being a thousand years old is still young. Do you understand?"

I stood up and she mulled that one over.

"Ok – it's sleep time now. Good ni…"

"How can someone live for ten thousand years?"

My mind was now firmly in the vineyards of Northern Spain, and I snapped.

"Because he's bloody magic!" I said, and began walking out of the bedroom door, until a wave of guilt pulled me back in.

"Look – we are going to have a brilliant Christmas, and Santa is not going to forget about you – or any other child, so stop worrying."

She smiled as I leaned in and kissed her on the forehead.

"Good night angel."

"Good night, Dad."

The door was not fully closed shut when she called out.

"Dad."

I paused and cocked my head to show I was listening.

"I didn't know whether to believe in him anymore at first, but I am glad he will be allowed to come still."

And with that she put her arm around her cuddly bear, turned on to her side and closed her eyes.

Banana Butter

"Mavis!"

I assertively knocked the glass on the door a several more times.

It was Saturday, and I hadn't seen her properly in five days. It had admittedly been getting progressively colder this week and I wasn't keen for her to come outside, but I needed to get her shopping to her.

She had a little porch at the front of her house. Not much more than a PVC frame built on to a small hard standing, it looked like a temporary structure that had been stuck-on to the front of the house as an afterthought. The PVC was a deep shade of green in many places where it had not been cleaned in years and was covered in algae. Each section of glass had condensation between the small, square panes, and there was black mould present inside, concentrated around the corners of the small room. Still, for the most part, it provided a suitably dry place to drop off Mavis' shopping.

She couldn't get out, and by her own admission, using a computer to order her groceries was beyond her – as it was for lots of 90-year-olds. She had a son, who lived in London now, whom I understood phoned sporadically, but there was no one else committed to looking after her. I had been bringing her shopping over for her since the first lockdown. And now we had entered the second wave, I had continued.

She only lived a couple of hundred meters away from me, in a nice little semi-detached house in a cul-de-sac at the end of my road. She had been friends with my Mum. They used to work together for years in a butter factory, and I had really gotten to know her well when I had taken summer jobs there before I started full time in the shoe shop.

Christ it was a depressing job. Measuring fidgety children's feet was a joy by comparison. I would always be put into a two-person team in the 'Returns' section. There would be no more than two teams operating at any one time, and we would all sit in a room on small wooden stools, next to a large metal drum (surprisingly not triggering the early onset of osteoporosis – for me, at least) and someone would wheel in a cart full of out-of-date butter. The kind that was in the foil wrapping. My job was to peel off the foil wrap, and then to lob the butter ten feet through the air, and into the drum, so that it could all be re-churned into 'fresh' butter again – somehow. I don't know what the rest of the process looked like, as I just got to see this one part, but I suspected it involved churning - on an industrial scale - and probably the addition of some food-safe chemicals.

The carts that they had full of this wrapped, out of date butter were apparently endless. We never, ever got to the end of it. They would just keep wheeling cart loads of it in. Neither were we ever aware of how much progress we had made on any given day. Nor was it disclosed what our expectations were. We just sat there – on these godawful uncomfortable stools, wrecking our backs – peeling off foil packaging and lobbing between 250 and 500 grams worth of its contents, through the air and into the large container. I could put up with it - it was only pocket money for me, but there was one bloke who had been doing it full time for 18 years.

Day in, day out for 18 years! Whatever God's purpose for putting this guy here on earth, surely it could not have been to just lob gone-off butter into a large drum for 8 hours a day? Maybe there was a significant moment that had passed or was yet to come. Perhaps he would save an orphan from a burning building, or do something else equally heroic, before returning to his calling that was tossing dairy products through the air with gay abandon.

Mum and Mavis worked together in the offices. They were in the sales team and responsible for taking orders from the supermarkets, the cash and carry's and the like – and no doubt facilitated the returns of the unsold butter to transform them once again into fresh butter. Interestingly, Mavis never put butter on her shopping list. Instead she always asked me to get the blackest bananas that the shop had. She had told me that these bananas mashed very well, and she would use this instead as a natural, butter substitute on her toast or in her sandwiches. In her sandwiches! Even if it was a cheese or ham sandwich! I used to think it was a sign of eccentricity, but she used to defend it by implying that I was the idiot and that the butter-spread they sold these days was just a few molecules in their structure away from being plastic.

This week, she hadn't asked for any bananas but weirdly had asked for a bottle of Jack Daniels. I didn't know she was a drinker – and even then, I would have expected her occasional tipple to be a Harveys Bristol Cream, rather than a smoky bourbon. She always left the cash inside the porch for me from the previous weeks shopping, so I didn't mind. I'd fetch her whatever she asked for.

I knocked the glass of the internal door again. The original 'front' door prior to the porch being installed over the top of it.

"Mavis! I got your shopping love. I just want to check that you're alright," I shouted through the letterbox, opening it up slightly with my thumb.

Still nothing. I stepped back outside the porch and looked up at the windows at the top of the house for any signs of life.

"She must be in there. I could hear her television set this morning," came a voice from behind me.

Oh, bloody hell. I should have known if I had stuck around that he'd soon be out, snooping.

"Hello Malcolm. How are you?" I asked politely.

He was an elderly man, early eighties I think Mavis had told me. He had been recently widowed only last year. And now, with no filter, had become even more meddlesome than he had been before.

"Well…." he began, followed by the taking in what felt like the slowest, deepest breath I had heard from behind his full-face protective visor. Whilst I waited for his considered reply, he ponderously took his gloved hands from his pockets and moved them to his hips. This was his battle stance. I would struggle to get away for a while now.

"Well you know. Can't grumble."

Ah shit. That could only mean one thing. He had plenty on his mind he intended to grumble about to me. I intervened before the rant began.

"Have you seen Mavis recently?"

"Well," he began again, unhurriedly, "I haven't seen anyone for a couple of weeks. Not properly. I talked to Sid last week over the back fence for ten minutes. He was telling me he's had a bumper crop of runner beans this year. Just finished harvesting them last week. In fact, he let himself in the next day when I was in the bath and kindly left a bag of them on the kitchen table for me. Lovely t–"

Sid was Malcolm's next-door neighbour on the other side of his property.

"But you said you've heard her?" I interrupted.

"Well..." Again, the pregnant pause. Christsakes!

"I did hear her TV on earlier this morning, yes. It was very loud, which I thought was a bit strange as I don't normally hear it through the wall. Now Sid's," – he paused for a moment and performed the universally understood gesture hitch-hikers have used for decades, with his thumb gesturing towards his neighbours house on the other side, "his TV is always blasting away in there. He's always been the same."

"Have you heard her voice, or seen her come to the door for anyone else?"

Finally recognising my concern, without hesitating and with a sense of certainty, said, "No. I've not seen anyone else go in or out, and I haven't heard from her."

I nodded and turned around to look back at Mavis' house. I went from window to window looking for any signs of movement. All I could hope for was to see twitching curtains, as they were all drawn although this was not especially strange as Mavis had always liked to do this.

"I'm a bit worried to be honest. I haven't seen her since Monday – and even then, I just got a wave from the upstairs window. All I could really see was her silhouette."

Malcolm shuffled down the path at the front of his garden and joined me in looking up at each window on the front of her house.

"I've definitely heard her in there though – not just the TV. Sometimes I can hear footsteps or doors slamming shut."

I nodded and walked back up to her front door to try again. I gave her door several more firm knocks. Still nothing. I had brought her shopping in and placed it in its usual spot for her, next to a long since used umbrella holder. I turned back to Malcolm and shrugged my shoulders.

"I'm worried Malcolm. Something is not right. She could be ill or might have fallen."

"I've got a spare key. Would you like to use it?" I didn't realise that he had a spare, and I felt a wave of relief upon hearing this news. Although I remained unsure how he had a key in the first instance.

"You have a key? Oh yes please. We need to check up on her. Please can you fetch it?"

"Just a minute. I think it's in the kitchen," Malcolm said as he hobbled off with all the urgency that his legs allowed him these days.

Mavis had always been quite lucid, and I was not aware of any hearing problems that she suffered with either, so there is no way she wouldn't be able to hear me knocking and calling out to her. I stepped over the unruly herbaceous border beneath her front lounge window and cupping my hands on the window, peered in. The curtains were pulled tightly together and all I could see was the rear lining of them.

Malcolm had still not returned when I suddenly became aware of a barely audible, gentle brushing noise. It was coming from inside the porch. I froze and looked directly toward the apparent source of it in an attempt to home in on the sound – blocking out all else. I moved very slowly and deliberately back toward the porch to keep it in my sights. It was the slightest of noises, and I hoped it would continue for long enough to allow me to reach a vantage point that would reveal its origins.

As I softly stepped out in front of the entrance to the porch, I could see what was causing the sound. The temptation was to begin shouting again - pleading with Mavis to open the door - but I fought it. I was not sure what was playing out in front of me, but I figured that whatever was happening, it was incumbent upon me to remain patient; at least for the moment. Plus, Malcolm would be back any minute with the spare key.

I froze and maintained my position so that my movements would not reveal my presence and watched a small envelope being gently eased out through the letterbox, disturbing the draught excluding brush as it did. The narrow, decorative panes of glass in the door were frosted, and in the absence of any back-light flooding through the house I could not identify the silhouette on the other side of the door as being Mavis' with any degree of confidence.

The envelopes progress had been slow as though its handler was not in the peak of their physical prowess and was struggling with the conviction of the action. In due course, it had almost fully appeared through the letterbox before a final firm poke saw it drop to the ground. I quietly approached the door, still trying not to betray my presence. I didn't want to scare anyone, or make my visits become unwelcome or even traumatic. I would investigate the letter to see what it said and go from there.

I moved slowly and quietly to the door and keeping my eyes on the inset pieces of glass for movements, stooped down and picked up the letter. I stood back up before gently tearing the flap. It had been licked down but was still sticky and I was able to open it without making a tear.

I pulled out a small note contained within, written on a lined page torn from a very small notebook. It appeared to be a shopping list, but something immediately didn't sit right with me. As I stood studying it, drifting far away lost in my thoughts, I was jolted out of it by a voice right behind me.

"Well. I'm a bit stumped."

Malcolm had returned, with a face an equal mixture of embarrassment and bemusement.

"Where's the key?" I asked with some urgency.

"Well, that's the thing," he said, shaking his head slowly and dropping head down until he was staring down at his shoes. "I don't know."

"What do you mean you don't know?" I pressed.

He threw his hands out to the side and sheepishly looked back up at me.

"I just don't know where it is. It's been on my key hook in the kitchen since she gave it to me at sometime last year. I definitely haven't used it since March. I haven't really been out myself since then."

Disappointed, I looked back down at the shopping list. Malcolm peered over.

"What have you got there?"

"It's a shopping list. But there's something not right about it."

Mavis had always left her shopping list under a large shiny pebble in her porch when she was expecting me. Of course, she had been shielding and avoiding contact with anyone given her age, so she never came out and handed it to me personally. Though I did usually get a wave through a window when she heard me knock and leave the shopping – if she was awake. But it was very odd that she would feed the list out through the letterbox to me, and not then follow it up with a wave through the window.

"What's strange about it?" Malcolm enquired – putting his default nosiness to good use.

I stared at it for a second more, before I answered.

"I don't know. Probably nothing. It's just, well I've been doing her shopping for months now, and – some of these items I've not seen on here before and they've thrown me a bit."

Malcolm asked if he could take a look, but I refused. It felt inappropriate; as though I was breaching her privacy based on what I knew she had previously asked for, so I shook off my suspicions, folded the list up and put it in my pocket.

"it's fine Malcolm. It's just me worrying unnecessarily. She's obviously OK, just keeping herself safe in there."

I was almost convincing myself.

I looked up at Malcolm, "But please, take my number, if you find that key could you please give me a call? I'd like to check on her properly all the same. And if you see her –

or anything odd…. or anything at all, perhaps give me a call then too. Please."

Malcolm could see I was still concerned, and he just nodded. I rummaged around for a pen in my handbag and wrote my mobile number down on my Asda receipt from the groceries, passing it to Malcolm.

"Yes of course. I'll keep this number safe."

"Try and keep it safer than the house key ideally, if you could."

Malcolm agreed to, a bit red faced.

We both walked down Mavis' path and out through her small metal gate, carefully closing the gate behind us. I said goodbye to Malcolm and walked back home; my stomach was in knots.

I always followed my gut, and of the few moments in my life where I had chosen to ignore my instinct, I had always later regretted it.

Always.

The Cuckoo

'Finally. I thought the nosy bitch would never go.
Make sure you close the gate behind you…. that's it. Off
you fuck.'
I watched the busybody walking off down the road,
glancing behind her once or twice before shaking her head,
picking up her pace and disappearing out of view. I turned
my attention to the other one.
'And you, you meddling old prick. Hurry up now.'
I watched the old man retreating up his own garden path
next door more slowly, and stiffly. I was eager to get my
hands on the goods this week. I had asked for a bottle of
Jack Daniels – the honey flavoured one – this week, and she
hadn't disappointed so far. As soon as he was gone, I would
open the door, reach out and grab the bag.
As he reached his front door, he gingerly reached for its
handle and wrestled it open with an awkward grip that
betrayed his advancing arthritis, and it slowly swung open.
Rather than walking straight in, he turned his attention to
removing his face visor. It must have had a safety clasp that
was located to the rear of his head, and he once again began

fumbling around without any authority or precision as he attempted to release it and remove the visor.

'Fucks sake man! Just do it in the house will yu'?'

I hadn't had any kind of Jack Daniels for a long time – let alone the honey one. I normally stuck to the supermarkets own brand of whiskey – a lot cheaper.

I'm not sure if it was because I was anxious, but he didn't seem to be getting anywhere with it. At one point I almost instinctively shouted out to him to see if needed help!

I have lived next door to Malcolm for about 30 years. He was a decent sort. Bit of an old woman. Worse now that he was on his own and he didn't have any company.

'Hang on – I think he has it…. YES! It's off, now just…OH FOR FUCKS SAKE!'

I squeezed my eyes shut and tilted my head back in sheer frustration as – after finally releasing and removing the visor – Malcolm bungled his handling and spilled the facial covering on to the floor beneath him.

Now he wasn't able to bend down and pick it up.

'You soppy sod. Just kick it into the house!'

Malcolm's physical range seemed to be between 90 degrees (an upright, standing position – although it was a little stooped these days) and 70 degrees. Bending any further was a problem, and certainly not all the way to the ground. After pondering his options for a few moments with his hands on his hips, he reached inside the door and around to the right. Withdrawing his arm, I could see that he now brandished a walking stick that must have been previously resting against the wall.

He lifted it out to where he stood and began poking around at the visor with it, like he was playing some kind of bad funfair fishing game. He paused for a moment, and looked up and down the street, but there was no sign of the cavalry. A little way down the road, some noisy kids were consumed with playing on their bikes, but there was no one else around.

'You're not going in are you, yu' sod.'

I had been bent over, leaning on the windowsill, peering from behind the curtain through the nets, and I felt an immediate release in stiffness when I stretched out and stood up straight. I sighed to myself. The only way I would be able to pick up that shopping undetected is if Malcolm pisses off inside – and he isn't going anywhere until he's picked up his precious bloody mask. I knew this because I remember hearing the very long, boring story about how he had purchased it and what he had paid for it several times over the back fence.

I looked back outside. He was still poking it around again on the floor with his stick.

Okay.

I flipped the latch back across the front door and put my coat on which had been resting on the staircase. I walked through the passageway and into the kitchen. The tumbler I had got ready in anticipation of a glass of my sweet bourbon treat sat bemused and alone on the kitchen table. The two large cubes of ice already having lost their frosted, icy veneer, now just looked like blocks of sweating water.

I unlocked the rear door, and cautiously opened it. The back garden had been overgrown and unkempt for several years now. There was only one house that could feasibly have a vantage point that could overlook my route through this garden – and that was Malcolms, and he was out the front. Nonetheless, I carefully crept out of the house and as I made my way to the end of the garden, I stayed close to the fence that adjoined Malcolm's garden all the way down.

The latch at the top of the wooden gate to the rear of the property's boundary had become loose in the rotten wood and was barely still affixed. A mild wind would be enough to rattle it now, which would repeatedly – and frustratingly – knock against the equally as rotten frame. I released the latch, opened it ajar and peered out.

Beyond the garden, on the other side of the gate was a small concrete path. No more than 25 metres from end to end, it provided convenient rear access to three garages belonging to the three houses that backed on to the lane. Turn left out of this gate, and there was a set of steps that took you down to the garages. Turn right and walk along, and you would encounter another two back gates. The first one you would come across was Malcolms, next door, and then finally mine at the farthest end.

A quick look left and right revealed that nobody was out there. I slipped through the gate, pulling it gently shut behind me and then executed several long strides (if it weren't for my age, I could have called them leaps) on the balls of my feet in near silence, until I arrived at my own back gate.

I reached over the top and let myself in. I jogged up the path and down the side of my house, appearing in the front garden. I wanted eyes back on my shopping as soon as possible.

"Are you okay Mal?" I asked, as casually as I could. Although I was actually blowing out of my arse and my heart was racing.

Malcolm turned around towards me in a fairly robotic fashion. Upon realising that it was me, he smiled with relief.

"Oh Sid. Perfect timing. How are you?"

"I'm okay Mal. What are you doing there?"

"Well, I came out to talk to that young woman from down the road…." he paused, placed his hands on his hips and looked down at the ground, "now what's her name?"

He began to withdraw into a Zen-like state of concentration – tutting to himself every now and again.

I patiently waited for longer than was comfortable. Every time I attempted intervening with a comment designed to move the conversation on again, I was countered with, "it's on the tip of my tongue" or, "it'll come to me now." He had no equal when it came to being tediously digressive.

I tried again, more forcefully.

"What's that down there on the floor?"

"Jacqui!" he suddenly proclaimed, his head jerking bolt upright as the recollection of her name sparked him back into life.

"Oh. I'm not sure I know her," I lied.

"She has helped Mavis with her shopping for a long time now. Used to work together at some point, I think. Nice woman. Dark haired. Her husband is that bus driver. The Italian looking one with the round glasses. Looks like cross between Sylvester Stallone and Elton John."

"Yes, now I know her. Do you need …."

"So anyway, she was saying that she hasn't seen Mavis this week. At all. I haven't seen her either. Heard her TV once or twice, but nothing else. Have you seen her?"

This question to me felt quite pointed – made all the more dramatic by the silence that followed it. Or perhaps I was being a little too paranoid.

"Mavis? No. Not me. I don't spend anytime out the front of the house anyway. Usually tending to me beans out back. No not seen her for…well….it must be weeks."

I became conscious that my eyes were searching around everywhere as I replied. Before Malcolm had a chance to speak again, I thought I had better add the following by way of a hasty blurt:

"Is she ok?"

Malcolm nodded confidently.

"I think she's alright, yes. She's definitely in there, just a little bit more cautious than usual I would say."

As the words faded, I tried to get things back on track, and pointed at the visor on the floor.

"Let me help you with that Mal," I said.

"Ah – yes my face visor. Yes please Sid."

Getting to where the visor was in Malcolm's garden meant leaving my garden via the front gate and entering his. Before I even exited mine, a large white van pulled up on the kerb outside Mavis' house. The door flew open and out bounded a dishevelled looking young man, with wild and curly black hair wearing a pair of shorts that looked like jeans with the legs hacked off.

He walked to the rear of the van not taking his eyes off a small device that he was relentlessly tapping away at with a stylus, squeaking away like a pack of rats in the attic. He slid it back into a holster on his hip, opened the rear doors of his van and reached in for a large parcel.

When he produced it, it wasn't a cardboard box, but a decorative brown wicker basket with a suitcase type handle and two leather straps. I recognised what it was straight away. A food hamper. No doubt a gift from someone.

It looked quite heavy, and he needed both of his arms to carry it, managing with one only to open Mavis' gate for a brief second, before booting it wide open with his right foot. As he got to within a few meters of her front door, he nodded in acknowledgement as he noticed us watching. He placed it on her doorstep next to the shopping bags, retreated a few metres, and re-commenced bashing away at his handheld computer like a bohemian themed version of Al from Quantum Leap.

Malcolm couldn't help himself.

"I don't think she is taking visitors at the moment. If you leave it there, I will see that she gets it," he called across.

"Sorry pal need a signature," the young man said without looking up.

By now, I was in Malcolm's garden.

"Okay, can you just leave it with me instead?" he suggested.

The lad shrugged, as if to express he really couldn't give two shits what happened to it, in all honesty.

"No, it's okay. I'll sign for it." I swooped in and deftly picked up the visor, forcing it into Malcolm's hands, and gently nudging and guiding him into the direction of his house. "It's easier if I take it Mal, I know what your back is like."

The lad took one look up at the house for signs of movement, shrugged again, and went to gather the parcel to pass across to me.

"It's okay leave it there, just bring me the computer to sign," I asked, which he duly did, and – apparently satisfied – went back off down the path and into his van. A few seconds later, he had started it up, and after almost pulling out into the path of an oncoming vehicle, had gone.

"Ok Mal, you've got your visor now, you can head back indoors. I'll sort out th….."

I instinctively flinched and ducked as some kind of projectile whistled past my face. I heard the ball land in Mavis' garden and the voices of some young people laughing from behind me.

"Sorry Mister," one of them said, as he skipped over the garden wall to retrieve the ball. He was easily the tallest one. I put him at about 12 years old.

I stood back, Mal was looking flustered.

"Excuse me, you can't just go in there," he protested.

Completely ignoring him, the tall kids' eyes lit up when he saw the bounty of goods that lay outside Mavis' house.

"Boys! Come 'ere, look at this," he called out to them, and stood up frantically beckoning them over with his hand. Another five or six of them descended upon the garden like locusts, streaming through the gate one by one.

Marching over to the partition wall, I shouted, "Oi, get your ball and get out!"

The tall kid had now popped the hamper open and his eyes grew as big as saucers as he clocked the goodies inside. He went straight for the bottle of Prosecco and the brownies.

I raised my voice even further, genuinely pissed off that they were about to take something.

"Oi - you little bastards, get out of it. Gone on!"

69

In dribs and drabs, they ran out laughing. Until it was just the tall kid left. Bottle in one hand, packet of brownies in the other, he stood up straight, looked me in the eye, stuck his middle finger up at me, shouted 'fuck you' and ran off behind them.

"What is it coming to, eh. I'll go and tidy it up. Can't let Mavis do it. I bet she is in there, terrified," said Malcolm.

"No, Mal. Look, you go inside, and I will go and sort it out. No real harm done. She doesn't drink anyway."

"Are you sure Sid. I am a bit tired. I tend to get tired very quickly these days you know. I think it's.."

"Well in you go now, come on, put your feet up," I cut him down stone dead out of fear of another meandering story.

"Oh, well thank you," he began saying as I stood behind him as he began shuffling inside, until we were both startled by a call from behind us.

"Oh my God, what's gone on here?"

We both turned around to see Jacqui stood at the foot of Mavis' garden.

Steading the swinging gate from the boys' hasty exit with her hand, she surveyed the scene open mouthed. I hadn't noticed, but there were brownies strewn all over the garden and the hamper, with its lid thrown open, added to the disorder.

This was inconvenient.

"Oh hi, I was just about to tidy that up," I offered before being interrupted by Malcolm, who – annoyingly – began walking towards Jacqui, which meant in turn he was walking away from his house.

"Some boys did it. A lovely hamper was dropped off for Mavis, and these boys ran in, made a right mess and were very rude to us indeed. Sid was about to clear it up and keep it by for her."

Jacqui shook her head and crouched down to start picking up the mess.

"I know the little bastards," then looking at Malcolm, "I had to come back Malcolm. Something doesn't feel right. I had to see her."

My attempts to get Malcolm back in the house had become well and truly derailed now as he became fully engaged in Jacqui's mission.

"You're right. We need to see her."

Now I had a problem.

Jacqui marched up to the door – glancing down at the groceries she had recently left on the doorstep – and robustly knocked at the door.

"Mavis!"

More robust knocking.

"Mavis! Can you come down please?"

She took a few paces back, surveyed the windows, and stepped up again to continue the knocking and the shouting.

"Mavis!"

Of course, she got nothing back.

"Right, I'm calling the police," and as quick as a cat she whipped her mobile phone out of her pocket.

"Wait just a minute," I interjected. "Just before you do, let me nip around the back and call over her fence. She could be around the back or in the kitchen and not be able to hear us."

Jacqui clearly doubted this as a potential explanation but agreed to rule it out anyway.

Without appearing too keen, I hastily set off. I used the same route. Into my front garden, down the path, through the alley, out my back gate, along the path until I reached Mavis' back gate. I had to make this effective. I waited until I could hear that there was no traffic passing on the road at the front and called out as loud as I could.

"Mavis! Mavis! Are you there?"

I let a few seconds pass.

"Mavis! Is that you?"

Few more seconds. Wait for the road to be quiet.

"OK, I'm coming in."

I unlatched the gate and shut it behind me. There was a large breeze block nearby, and using my foot, I pushed it against the foot of the gate. I legged it up the path and tumbled into the kitchen through the back door – careful to lock it behind me with the key I had stolen from Malcolm's kitchen when I had let myself in to drop off the runner beans. The ice in my whiskey glass had now melted completely.

Racing up the passageway, I kept low to the ground and turned to go up the staircase. I knew I needed to pull out all of the stops now, or my number was up. I would have to go in the front bedroom.

I had wanted to gag from the foot of the stairs. Even at that distance, the power of the smell was incredible. A car with this level of odour after an accident would have been written off by the insurance company. When I opened the door, it was so much worse.

It hit me in a wave. The same as how the heat had hit me when I stepped off a plane after it had landed in Spain. It got into my throat, and I could somehow taste it. The gases that had been emitted all brought their own unique odour to this most potent of cocktails. It smelt like a rubbish tip on a boiling hot summers day where the garbage is fermenting, coupled with a few drops of a sickly sweet, cheap perfume. Without even realising it was about to happen, I vomited in my mouth and swallowed it back down. The acid stuck to, and burned, the back of my throat.

I was suddenly reminded of my expectant audience. As well as being willed on to find some clean air, I upped the pace and fought through it.

The wardrobe was on the far wall and I stormed over to it, almost ripping the doors off their hinges. Swiping the hung clothes on the rail left and right with undisciplined abandon, a pale blue nightdress caught my eye.

'That should be easy enough to just put over my head.'

So keen to rid the smell of mothballs away from up my nose, in my haste, I ripped a hole in the armpit as I scrambled it on.

'The hair. How can I conceal the hair?'

I ripped open the top drawer in a chest of drawers nearby, tossing everything out as I reviewed the contents. Nothing. I glanced out of the window. Malcolm was stood with his hands on his hips looking the house up and down. Jacqui had her arms folded in a more impatient looking stance, still cradling her mobile phone. I checked the next drawer, flinging items all over the floor. My stomach continued to turn.

Aha. That will do. I reached for the towel and wrapped it around my hair. Ok, hope this cuts it.

I hunched my back up, and slowly and lamely walked over to the window. I pulled the net curtain ever so slightly to the side and waved. I hoped that from below they would be able to see an arm in a pale blue nightdress feebly waving down at them, but the net curtain would obscure my identity from being revealed.

Malcolm waved back at me. Jacqui had raised her arm to wave but had never entirely followed through. She was not convinced. Shit. I did not have time for this. I had to get out of this room. I couldn't take much more of the smell.

I withdrew my waving arm slowly and arranged the net curtain back into place, when Jacqui began motioning towards me. It was a beckoning type of gesture, but it had a rather demanding nature to it. The movements were sharp and insistent. She was almost ordering me downstairs.

From behind the net curtain, I shook my head rigorously, so it was visible, but this did not satisfy her. She looked back down at her mobile phone and dialled a very short number before putting it to her ear and staring back up at me. Right in the eye. A mixture of intense nervousness came over me and coupled with the pungent smell I was enveloped by, I projectile vomited against the window.

Alarm bells rang. Jacqui shouted something down the phone and ran for the door. She began hammering it relentlessly this time, shouting 'open up'. I panicked. I needed to flee. I spun around, slipping in the puke that lay all around me and slammed down on my back on to the floor, taking the wind out of me.

I must have lay there for up to a minute, dazed and intoxicated from the stink that I was at the epicentre of. The screaming and banging of Jacqui trying to break down the front door was soon drowned out by the sounds of the approaching police sirens. Within seconds it was upon me, and at least two patrol cars screeched to a halt on the road outside the house.

I just lay there on the bedroom floor, looking up at the ceiling and waited for them to come.

I was looking forward to my evening meal made from this weeks shopping. I had asked for asparagus tips, fresh kale and of course I had some of my very own runner beans as accompaniments. For dessert, a salted caramel cheesecake.

But I would not be having an old friend for dinner tonight.

Deceptive Simplicity

Martin was so slow. Even the simplest of instructions needed to be explained several times. I was all for giving youngsters a chance, but this kid was one of the worst apprentices I'd had through. Still can't complain. He wasn't costing me anything at present, so it didn't really matter.

"Martin, can you go and get the lighting out of the van please. We'll set it up in that corner. Stick it over there for a minute before we bring the furniture in."

Though he had a mask on - so I could not confirm for sure - I imagine that beneath the mask he was open mouthed as he nodded to acknowledge the order. I remained sceptical as to where it would actually get erected.

For the purposes of this photoshoot, I had been fortunate that one of my close friends had a brother-in-law who was the caretaker of a local secondary school. We'd actually played poker together a couple of times as part of a bigger group. I only had to slip him fifty quid too. The school had two buildings - a 'new' one and an 'old' one. The new one was built in the 1970's so goodness knows when the old building was built – but it would be a perfect location for my shoot. Just got two hours before he returns to kick us out so that he can lock up – need to get a move on.

It wasn't the normal kind of commission that I would do, but at the moment, I'm happy to take any kind of work I can get my hands on. I lost about 25 wedding jobs last year, and my studio was closed for almost seven months. I've run my own business for fifteen years now, so I did manage to get some support, but my money was way down – and some of what I did get needed to be paid back one day. I also managed to keep Martin in a job. In fact, it was extremely lucky the furlough scheme had been extended or I probably would've had no choice but to give him the chop by now.

"No…I said the other corner." For crying out loud.

"Gently for Christ sake!" He had definitely been lucky. "Wire it up and I'll work on the set."

I had brought out the clock from the car already, needed to find somewhere to hang it. A visible clock was a critical part of it. I fished the two AA batteries out of my shirt pocket and popped them into the back of the clock and set the time to 1:25. It was only mid-afternoon, so there was still enough natural light coming through the doors at the end of the hall. Combined with our own lighting to enhance it slightly, that'll be perfectly credible.

I affixed some thick and strong double-sided tape to the back of the clock and stuck it to the wall. Just needed it to stay in position until I captured the pictures I needed, then I could easily remove it before we left. It looked good, and the position would serve as the centre point for the framing of the shots.

Martin had arranged the lights and plugged them in, and now stood idly around, picking his nose. "Martin. Can you get my camera bag and tripod from the car, please?"

He trotted off back to the car. He had brought the van down with all the equipment and props, and I had driven down separately. Earlier on this morning, Martin had loaded the van at our studio while I went on to meet the caretaker and began scouting the shot out. Hopefully, he had remembered everything.

I was planning on using a normal, general purpose lens. It needed to have a 'natural' quality to it – almost as if it were a snapshot that had been taken on a phone. Important to not look like it was professionally done. The wide aperture of the normal lens meant that they were ideal for indoor photography. I would run some kind of filter on it later during post-production – possibly even give it a slightly grainy quality. I will get a few shots on my iPhone too, from a few different angles. They could easily be used across different territories then. That reminds me – I must cover up any plug sockets with props. That would be a dead giveaway if they were to be used outside of the UK.

Martin had returned and passed me my camera bag and tripod.

"Thanks. Ok – let's head back to the van and get the star of the shoot out!" He didn't laugh – not even out of politeness and/or due deference towards his boss – but I smiled to myself anyway.

We walked back down the hallway and outside to where our van was parked. We only had a few steps to ascend to get it back into the building, and it was on wheels so could be pushed once inside. Shouldn't be a problem.

I had been given the budget that allowed me to go for total authenticity with the props. I was approached in the same way that I picked up many of my jobs, through my Facebook page. Though this was the only aspect of the assignment that could have been described as 'typical'.

It was late one evening. Helen had gone to bed, and I was up watching The Crown on Netflix. Helen thought it was a bit boring, so I always waited until she went to bed. Just as I was thinking about joining here, there was a loud ping as my mobile phone provided notification that I had received a message.

Some bloke that I had no mutual friends with – in fact, I noticed that he barely had any friends at all – had messaged me. This wasn't completely out of the ordinary, it was just that so much of my business came from word of mouth, during gaps in dialogue with the potential client, it was always something I would check out.

The first message had simply asked whether I would be up for some 'bespoke still life work', and the vague inference that it would be well rewarded – so long as I kept the details of the job confidential. I said I was interested – but that of course I needed more information to be able to decide for sure.

He instantly replied by telling me that the job would be worth £5,000 to me – which he would pay up front and transfer straight to my account upon agreement. Then, I would be given a strict deadline by which time the photos were to be finished and submitted. No later than this they would need to be uploaded to Dropbox, and a link sent to some generic looking Yahoo address. He told me that no invoice or receipt would be required but reiterated that there were just three points of paramount importance.

The first was that the details of the job were to be kept completely confidential – before and after it was completed - and the second was that the photos had to look completely authentic. And do not watermark the photographs with anything pertaining to my business or identity. This was effectively tantamount to surrendering the copyright, but for that rate of pay, they would be welcome to it.

He then told me that he was just a middleman working on behalf of some very wealthy clients of his but not without imparting some rules of engagement, during which I sensed some threatening undertones. He informed me how nothing less than completing the job to the exacting standards - as would be specified - and completely in line with the deadlines given were crucial, and that his clients would be closely following my progress. I replied saying I was interested, but that I was getting a little concerned about the legality of this job.

He told me that I would not be asked to do anything illegal, or be compromised in any way, and asked me to confirm my acceptance of these terms; that time was of the essence. If I agreed I would be paid within 24 hours, and the job was to be completed within 72 hours.

I have a family. My money was down for the year. I wasn't sure when I would start getting work coming back in; when weddings could be booked again. I needed that money. It was all a little shady – and maybe a little bit too good to be true – but I had no hesitation in confirming that yes, I would accept those terms.

He gave me a description of what he wanted me to and asked me to make notes. It sounded easy enough to be honest. He made some specific points that I should pay attention to, and over the course of a 10 minute message based chat, I was pretty clear on what I needed to do. He gave me the email address that I needed upon completion of the job and asked me twice if I had noted it down – asking me to check it over thoroughly. He asked me for my bank details, there and then – which I gave him – and said something like 'the clock starts ticking when the money hits my account'.

I can't go back and read the conversation over again because as soon as he had given me enough chance to read this last line, he left the chat – and closed his account. I haven't been able to find him since.

My head was spinning at the time – mainly out of excitement about the thought of picking up the unexpected payday. It all happened so quickly. I can remember his first name was Sam, and his photo was of the bronze Lady Justice statue outside the Old Bailey in London – holding her sword aloft. Also, his surname began with an F. Ferryman? Fernley? Fenner?.... I searched them all but couldn't find a trace.

I headed up to bed but found that I couldn't sleep a wink now. As soon as I cannot sleep, I start thinking. And the more I think about things, the inevitably increased brain activity just perpetuates my inability to nod off. I think it was about 3am before I was finally able to get some sleep. It was the same principle when I awoke about five hours later. As soon as I recalled the unconventional procurement of my services the night before (which was within the first ten seconds of opening my eyes), my heart started beating faster, and my brain went on high alert.

I had grabbed my discarded trousers on the floor next to me and fumbled around to find the pocket which contained my phone. Bugger, it was dead. I leapt up and grabbed my dressing gown from the back of our en-suite bathroom door and went racing down the stairs to find my charger in the lounge. I can still picture the kids' bemusement on their faces as I barked 'Morning' at them whilst frantically looking behind cushions and chairs for my charger.

When I found it, I plugged it into the wall in the kitchen and boiled the kettle to make a coffee. I didn't end up making one though. As the little corporate jingle that played automatically upon start-up faded away, I opened the banking app for my personal account and let out a loud 'SHIT!' which sent my two kids running out the kitchen to see what was wrong.

I'd been paid my five grand. At 6am this morning. That meant the first two hours had passed, but to be honest, once I stopped to think about it, the job still didn't faze me – and I could always just work two hours later tonight. I wasn't sure who Sam's clients were, but at this price I didn't care too much.

"Martin – you go inside the van and grab the far end. I'll take this end."

I wanted to make sure it wasn't dropped on to the tarmac and damaged to be honest!

I'd picked it up on eBay. It was in a 'used' condition – and had it been for personal use I think I would have left it well alone – but for this job it was perfect. It looked faded, scratched, and generally grimy – and it only cost me 300 quid.

"OK, I'm lifting …. NOW. Push it along to me. That's it, that's it," I said as I brought it gently down to the ground. Martin jumped down and lowered down the back end.

"That's it, now you go first up the steps….1, 2, 3, LIFT."

It went up the few steps and into the building easily enough.

"OK. I'll wheel it down to situate it. You go back and get the trolleys too." Martin nodded.

I pushed it down the hall and set it up against the wall just beyond where I had placed the clock, clicking down the brakes on the wheels with my foot. I stepped back ten paces or so to view the whole shot. Yes, that looked pretty good. We had two trolleys that Martin was bringing in. In them I had packed a box containing clip boards, what appeared to be paperwork and blue roll that we would use to make them look like a 'working' trolley. On one end of each of them, we had a few squirty bottles that we had filled up with different coloured liquids, and we had hung them by their triggers over the handle. A mop leant up against it finished the look. I had just the places in mind that I could position them. One in the background beyond the clock, and one in the foreground – mostly out of shot.

All looking good. Get a few shots and get out of here. Now I'm here, and ready to go, I've got this weird nervous feeling in my stomach.

I know what I'm doing is a bit suspect – but that's not for me to worry about? I've been given a job to complete – a job that pays incredibly well - and I need the money. I can't be held responsible for whatever someone does with the photos. And that goes for any photographs I've taken over the years. On any photo I take, there's always a chance that the copyright could potentially be infringed by the client.

But with the client paying such a high price, the confidentiality clause, and stipulating no watermark, to me it seems implied that they want the copyright to the photos. This was not something I wished to have a conversation about to clarify. In any case – there was no one I could get hold of to talk about it. Nope – I would stick to the plan. Take the photos, edit, upload, and send on the link. Delete all imagery that can link any of it to me and forget this ever happened.

The situation with this new strain of COVID is worrying. The mutant offspring surging through the UK is universally considered to be significantly more contagious. Up to 70% more so I heard. It replicates in the throat. Since its discovery cases have soared. New, unwanted records were being broken every week. Infections. Deaths. Highest number of COVID related hospital admissions.

The NHS were reporting that the situation regarding hospital capacity, and the dwindling number of trained specialists was more dire than at any other time in this crisis. Even than right back at the start of it in March and April 2020.

The radio phone in shows, news channels and newspapers were full of irate Doctors and NHS staff imploring the general public to heed their warnings. To stop acting irresponsibly. Follow the basics – wear a mask, socially distance, wash thoroughly. If you don't – you will have blood on your hands. Even if you were fortunate enough to not get ill, you could be a carrier and pass it on to someone who could die. The messages were clear.

And if these warnings weren't stark enough, it was nothing compared to the sort of contempt that they held in reserve for the COVID deniers. The ones who would hold protests with no regard for social distancing; who would spray paint the sides of bridges along motorways with phrases like 'Fake Pandemic' or 'Coup 19'. And the ones who champion the 'Great Reset' conspiracy theory about the pandemic. These people were held in the highest level of disdain, and constantly told that they could be responsible for changing behaviours and attitudes that will result in killing other people. And of course, they could, it was true.

This wasn't the same though. Was it?

Don't lie to yourself. You know what they are doing.

But if not me, it would be someone else. I wouldn't be solving anything.

It's not for me to say. After all, it's not the actual gun that's the problem. It's the potential recklessness of the person who fires it. And I was only guilty of owning the gun.

Just be professional. Focus.

It can't be for me to.....

"Ah there you are Martin. Just wheel the trolleys up here."

Martin had one small trolley per hand, and he had loaded them up with the other stuff from the van too.

"Great, you bought the sheets too. Good thinking."

I walked toward him to relieve him of the trolleys and to position them in the shot.

"You take the sheets and the pillows and put them on the bed."

Martin scooped the linen up and took them over to the bed that lay in the middle of our hallway set.

"Martin, can you drop the side bars down – they would only be in the up position, in theory, if there was a patient in it. Oh – and the back tilts. Tilt it upward so that it is at about a 45-degree angle – more of a sitting up position than a laying down one."

As I arranged the trolleys, I watched Martin wrestling with the lever that controlled the angle of the bed. He eventually got it. Yes, that looked much better.

"Martin, when you are putting the sheets on the bed, there's no need to actually make the bed. Sort of half tuck the sheets in at the bottom, and have the rest strewn across the top. Our client wants to communicate a sense of disorganisation in his campaign. Then turn the lighting on, and we'll get the pictures."

I stood back and checked the shot. Looks great. The hallway stretched on for about 100 feet and was well lit. Apart from our props – which set the scene – it was empty.

God Hates The Fall

It's so windy, I can't stand still
I'm getting pushed and shoved around
It's biting my coarse, rough skin and making it sore
It is as though I am at a Slayer concert

My hair is thrashing around all over the place
And the wind is making a steady droning sound
Like Kerry King feeding his guitar back against his custom
Marshall amp
It is raining too
And when the wind blows through the gap in the
corrugated garage roof
It sounds like the applause of a distant, yet vast, audience
But I am far away, and the festival has forgotten me

I haven't seen Brian in days
He's a naughty little so and so
It's too cold out here at the moment
We had a few people over on Bonfire Night
Don't think we were supposed to

We let off some fireworks – and the Catherine Wheel left
me scarred
  Brian strolled around all night like the bollocks
  Firing off precision punts
  Cleanly kicking off his little cousins' mittens

I like to look across the garden, over the fence and toward
the mountain
  It is covered in trees until about two thirds up
  Then from there to the mound at the top, it is as bald as a
coot
  There are three Bronze Age burial sites at the top
  I've always wanted to go up and see them, but I can't

There's someone coming to see me today
  A kind of Doctor I think
  He drives a van that says Surgeon on the side anyway
  He's already been here and sized me up
  Frowning and tutting and grinning
  I am scared
  There's not anything wrong with me, you see
  But he has everyone believing that there is

I hear a car driving our way
  The street is quiet, everyone tends to stay inside now
  It comes into view, and I can see that it is not a car
  It's a tipper truck
  The truck slows down on approach
  It is the same Doctor as before on board
  Driving it along

He goes past our driveway and begins turning it around
It looks like he's going back the way he came
Perhaps they changed their mind and sent him away
A bright white light blinks on, and the truck starts moving
backwards instead
Backwards on to our driveway

Our driveway is on a slope
As it moves into position, I can see inside the flatbed
What I see fills me with dread
I feel sick and the fear cripples me
I start counting to ten to calm down
I cannot run – I am rooted to the spot
The wind falls silent

The flatbed is full of limbs
Limbs that have been cut off
Unsympathetically tossed into the back
Strewn all over and piled up on top of one another

Some of the cuts look rough and crude
A lack of precision work is evident
Like the act of a butcher
A fiend
And now they all lay there
Like a Nazi Doctor's offcuts
Failed experiments, bound only for the furnace

The Surgeon is talking to my family from about 6 feet away
I can only see the backs of their heads
Nodding now and again

I can't see their faces but I somehow know they are weeping
As they consent to the guidance being doled out
From my apparent Angel of Death

Grave faced but stoic
The Surgeon drops the tail of the tipper
He reaches in, groping around between the hacked off limbs
Rummaging around he finds his device of dismay
What has wrought such carnage
A chainsaw
The remains of his previous victims still caked into the teeth

Checking it over one last time
The vendor of atrocity begins his approach
This would be my last season
Before the inevitable abyss

The side alley gate is thrown open
A rock pushed up against it with his boot
He swaggers his way over to me slowly
Relishing every step
Taking as much enjoyment from the anticipation
As he no doubt will from the act itself

I realise I have been holding my breath
I release it and get an instant headrush as I draw new
Or it could be the smoke of the cigarette
That is hanging out of the corner of his mouth

He flashes a malicious smirk, stepping right up to me
And he removes it and I wince as he stubs it out on my body

He pushes the throttle trigger on his weapon
It snarls into life
The visceral sound drives deeply into my being
The chaotic and fateful noise filling the air
I have been condemned
And my fate preordained
He raises the chainsaw

The first cut rips into me
But he does not immediately withdraw
He holds it there, pressing it inward
The agony fills my body
All I can see is white light
All I wanted to do was provide

Seconds later
The sonic presence of his instrument subsides
The pace of the waves and vibrations decelerate
And there is a dull thump
As my first limb lands on the wet grass beside me
Callously it is kicked aside by his steel toe-capped boot
And the chainsaw is cranked up again

I glance up to the skies
As limb number two is lined up with the guide
In the upstairs bedroom I can see a silhouette
The wind blows wildly one last time

As though it is rallying in support of me
I flail dangerously in this gust
Raging at my supposed protectors
As the blinds are sharply flicked shut

Both momentary and endless
Constantly excruciating
And utterly incapacitating
Being shown no mercy
My energy is sapped, as I am dissected
More body parts to be added to my tormentors stack

But from these killing fields
I am looking forward to the green pastures
And still waters
I will fear no evil
I will be admitted to the garden of paradise
And live there instead

The Club

Life is different now. Everyone told me it would get easier, but it hasn't. People ask me how I'm doing, and I tell them something like, "Not bad," or "Getting there," but I'm only saying what I think people want to hear – or what I think they will be comfortable with hearing. That's all they really want me to say - so we can move past it and just have a normal conversation anyway. I don't blame them – Christ, how can anyone start a conversation with me at the moment that doesn't acknowledge it. It's just something we have to touch base with, and then it's in everyone's interests to quickly move past it.

I've got a couple of close friends - or my brother - if I really needed to talk about it, but to be honest, it suits me as well. Glossing across the surface of it is the only way I feel confident that I will be able to hold it together. Over the last few weeks, I've expanded my stock answers to say, "Shall I answer that how I normally answer it, or do you want the truth?". It was an evolution really. I just needed something new to say to people - especially the ones I see at work on a daily basis, who have seen my routine.

I was just a few years off retirement; mortgage had been paid off a couple of years ago. We had looked forward it - and the prospect of spending more time together. We loved our little UK caravan breaks. Newquay was our favourite place. We were always on the internet looking for deals on caravan holidays. It didn't matter whether it was a Gold, Silver or Stone level of trim, we just loved getting down there; walking along the front; having a drink in the club; listening to the heavy rain hitting the metal roof like rounds popping off from a Tommy gun. We didn't go abroad really – Jan didn't like flying, and we always used to say, 'why bother spending the extra when you've got everything you need within a few hours' drive!' And if you've got the weather, then there's truly nowhere better anyway.

I have two sons. The older one is married with his own kids – my two grandsons – and off living his own life. They aren't very local anymore – and with the lockdown restrictions I have only seen them a few times this year. When we cautiously began exiting the first lockdown and things eased up for a bit, the whole family came and visited me, and we sat together in the garden for a few hours. It was nice. Apart from the youngest one, Danny, who kept asking if Nanny's headache was better so she could come outside and see him. He was only four – we couldn't tell him yet.

My younger son lives at home – well his driving licence says so and his bank statements come to this address – but he works long hours, he runs a lot, he's courting…. he's doing all the things he should be doing at his age. He will arrange to take me out for the odd pint or bit of pub grub –

and he even makes some of them too instead of cancelling on me at the last minute! It's fine; really.

I have entered this weird zone where I am aware of myself more. I feel like I live in a bubble and I am more conscious of what is playing out before me. I no longer have an auto-pilot setting. I analyse each human interaction, whereas I mostly used to – sometimes dismissively - take them at face value. I think it's part of the grieving process. I can't think as straight as I used to, and my disrupted mind is having to re-learn some of these social protocols. And it's made more complicated now.

When the first lockdown happened, and we all simultaneously clapped outside, were encouraged to 'be kind', and everyone was pulling together, I thought the 'Blitz spirit' would prevail and help pull us out the other side. Unfortunately, the opposite seems to be true. Since the first lockdown, it seems as though everyone is even more hell-bent on hanging one another for the tiniest of personal gain to themselves. I could understand it in the people who had faced the biggest challenges – perhaps financial, or health-wise, but as per, in my experience these were the people who would typically show the greatest humility and humanity.

These were the people who would not think twice about writing a trite letter of complaint as they felt that there was an opportunity to take financial advantage of a situation, for example – despite their Facebook posts during the pandemic encouraging everyone to 'shop local' and support local businesses. These were the people who were leaving shitty reviews on Google for the barely surviving bar – complaining that the bar staff would not come across to their table to pour their bottle of wine they had purchased into a glass for them each time. These were the friendly neighbours who would sympathise with you that lockdown had been mentally challenging, and then shop you to the police when you have a friend over in the back garden because you need to talk to someone. People seem more hypocritical and bitter than ever. Or maybe it's just because of the frame of mind I am in at the moment.

I do think that it's always been there to a greater or lesser extent; perhaps I just never used to notice it. But I do now. Since she went, it sometimes feels like I'm looking down on things happening to other people. And sometimes it can be in slow motion too. It does come with its advantages. I now find that I'm able to gather my thoughts more calmly and articulate myself better. It helps when I'm in situations that involve talking to other people - mainly strangers. There was a right beauty in Asda today, for example.

I was stood at the front of the store – adjacent to the kiosk where they sold the lottery tickets and cigarettes – and I had picked up a newspaper. Strictly speaking, I shouldn't have, but I have a habit of slipping into a bit of a trance like state just recently – and I think I did it without thinking. So, while on autopilot, I started leafing through the pages, and scanning through the news stories. All of a sudden, I heard a heavily accented, Welsh, woman's voice. I didn't think she was speaking to me at first, so her words didn't burst my bubble until she repeated herself – much more loudly.

"Excuse me!"

I lowered the newspaper and looked over at her, no more than 10 yards away. She was a woman probably in her late 30's. Her lank, greasy hair lay across her pallid cheeks like seaweed on a clam, and her resting face was a look of exasperated annoyance.

"Are you talking to me?" I asked, slightly confused – glancing around in my immediate vicinity.

"Yeah you," she said as she motioned toward the newspaper I was holding. "Are you planning on buying that?"

I looked around to check we were not amassing an audience or making a scene.

"What's it got to do with you?" I calmly asked.

"Well, you're handling it, you're putting your germs on it," she indignantly snorted.

"I'm not coughing all over it. I've just picked it up to decide whether I'm going to buy it. Seriously, what's it to you anyway?"

"I don't want to catch your germs, do I?" the woman sarcastically replied – before adding without the merest hints of irony, "And I'm supposed to be shielding."

"Well, if you're that worried then, really, you shouldn't have come out. Why are you out?" I patiently asked – the old me wouldn't have given this considered answer and just told her to eff off.

Without hesitating or displaying any shred of self-awareness she dramatically put her hands on to her hips, scrunched her face up to the point that her lips resembled a dogs puckered up arsehole, and after stringing together some fairly deft side-to-side head movements with her painted-on eyebrows raised, hit me with:

"Because I needed to buy some fags – not that it's any of your business!"

I laughed out loudly ('HA-HA!') – replaced the paper back on the rack and walked out of the store chuckling and shaking my head. This self-righteous declaration amused me no end. It was like – to her mind – she had this winning card to play this whole time; a card fit to win any argument. If she had been holding a mic at this point, she not only would have dropped it, but would have performed a flossing victory dance like a slovenly-looking Fortnite character that had been unlocked upon purchase of the 'Nosy Wanker' upgrade pack.

Me and Jan would have laughed all the way home talking about that.

Jan…

It was the first day – the very first day – following the news that my work, classed as non-essential, would be closed for a period of lockdown, that it happened. Unbeknown to us at the time, it was the last time she would ever be home.

I had worked my last day on March 23rd, and was told that until further notice, I was not to come in to work. It crept up on us so suddenly – and I think everyone only thought it would last for a couple of weeks, but of course it didn't. It was the following day that while we were jet-washing the drive off together, Jan had said she felt a bit weak and light-headed. At the time, I didn't think too much of it and told her to go and have a cup of tea with a few sugars in it.

As she went into the house, I could hear her panting for breath – which did get my attention. I turned off the jet washer, and made my way over to her, but I couldn't get to her in time. Before she could get to the back door, she collapsed in front of me and struck her head on the step. I carried her into the house, lay her on the sofa and dialled 999.

I described the symptoms to them, and I could tell by some of their leading questions that they suspected it was a heart attack. I suppose this increased the category level and an ambulance did arrive within 40 minutes. While we waited, she was in and out of consciousness and not making much sense. I had already got a pack of aspirin from the first aid pack in the kitchen and had encouraged her to chew it up.

I couldn't travel with her in the ambulance - because of the Covid-19 restrictions in place. I couldn't visit afterwards for the same reason.

When she got there, I was told that she had been put into a Coronary Care Unit (CCU) and that the next 48 hours would be critical, and she would be monitored closely. I was promised two calls a day – one after the Doctor's morning and evening rounds after he'd had a chance to review the treatment and progress.

On average I would get one call a day and have to chase the other one for varying reasons – but everything seemed to be going to plan. They told me that within around 5 or 6 days she would be able to come home. A procedure to insert stents may be necessary at some later stage, but nothing too dramatic. Things changed though, and none of this happened.

On the twentieth day they scheduled a 'Face Time' call between us, which I was looking forward to. Unfortunately, it was a deeply saddening occasion. Not because it didn't transpire – it did – but because it will forever provide me with a lasting memory of the final time that I would see her alive. She was struggling to communicate with me and looked tired and frustrated. There was something I could not put my finger on at the time that felt different. We had been together for more than 40 years, and I knew something was profoundly wrong. At the time I was just living in hope, and a bit of denial. With the benefit of hindsight, I can now see that a certain quality she always had in spades – a spirit – was not there anymore. People probably think that about me a little bit now.

But I do have one thing that keeps me sane. Keeps me grounded.

Obviously, I have my family who I couldn't be without. I enjoy all kinds of sport and love going fishing. I enjoy listening to the '70's show' on Planet Rock radio.

But there is one thing that always puts a smile on my face and makes me feel normal for a few hours no matter how I am feeling.

The Club.

It was built sometime in the 60's – in the middle of a council estate. I remember when it opened. On the weekends the fellas would be queueing down the street to get in to watch the rugby, or some other sport in the bar. Then, later that afternoon, they'd go home for an hour to change - maybe put a shirt on – and in the evenings they'd be back queueing up outside again. But this time they'd have the wife in tow and would be queueing to get a seat in the lounge to play bingo and then later watch the singer.

It started out as a Labour club, which was common in this kind of location where lots of working-class people live – although I was never politically motivated myself. Nor was anyone I bothered with either. The club used to be a membership only venue, and it also meant that members could then enjoy slightly subsidised beer. Although the membership fee was negligent, when I joined, not only did I have to present myself and be interviewed before an appointed committee (no less than six blokes firing questions at me, I think), but I even had to be put forward, and recommended by an existing member to even get to that stage!

The brewery sold it about ten years ago to some bloke who basically just wanted the land to build a block of apartments on, I think. Thankfully, the brewery didn't agree to sell him the land it was on, so he only had the option of keeping it running as a business. They did let him re-invent it as a 'Sports Bar' – which went down quite well actually, as there was no need for membership anymore and some of the dated, unnecessary ceremony that came with it.

I think he thought he would play the long game with acquiring it. Get his foot in the door and he would be top of the list if the brewery ever did decide to sell but so far, thankfully, there's no sign of that. Especially as in the last few years, it's seen something of a revival in its fortunes. I think more people feel disenfranchised and are wanting some good old-fashioned community spirit and togetherness back.

My most recent routine over the last few years, was that every Friday straight after work, I would go up and meet a couple of the boys and play snooker. I'd leave about ten and get a bag of chips on the way home. On a Saturday, me and Jan would go up together and watch the singer.

The thing I love about it is that it doesn't matter what day or time I want to go up there. Whenever I go, there is always, always someone that I can go and sit down and have a chat with. And whoever it is, they are always pleased to see me.

The first time I went up there since Jan passed was tough. She was as much part of the scene as me though, so it helped because we could grieve together. As soon as I walked through the door, Bev came steaming over to me and give me a big hug and a kiss. She didn't say anything – and neither did anyone else say anything about what was a clear breach of the two-metre rule.

As she pulled back from me, she rubbed my arm and said, "You'll never stop hurting, love, but you will learn how to manage it." That was the first time I cracked in public. If anyone knew, it would be her. She had lost her daughter three years before in a road accident.

Terry came across – one of my many snooker sparring partners. Recently retired from working on the railway lines, he was a thick set man with huge forearms. Although imposing, he had a gentle but firm and reassuring deep voice. And – I wasn't the person who first noticed this – but dazzling, bright blue eyes, which juxtaposed itself against the potential brute force that he otherwise embodied.

"If you ever want to just talk, then I will sit there for an hour and just listen."

"Thanks Terry."

He winked back at me.

"So, what happens if I want to talk for more than an hour."

He sipped from his pint as he considered the question.

"Well, I'll just fuck you off. An hour's your lot."

We both smiled and bumped fists before he quietly slipped off back to the bar.

Idris was next. I don't know why we all called him Idris, as his name was John, but across he came in his woolly hat and a scruffy pair of faded blue tracksuit bottoms. He hadn't worked since he'd had a breakdown ten years ago.

"How are you pal? You bearing up?"

"Hiya Idris. Taking it day by day mate," I replied trying hard not to notice what looked like fragments of radioactive cheese he was storing between his crumbling teeth.

"I know exactly how you feel pal; how awful it is. I felt exactly the same way when I lost Dawn."

I have to be honest, my half-smile turned into a bit of a scowl upon hearing this.

"What the fuck do you mean – 'when you lost Dawn'?" I barked.

I turned slightly so that I was fully facing him.

"She's in the fucking lounge next door - playing bingo! You can walk through that door and go and see her now if you want. If I want to go and see mine, I've got to go to the fucking cemetery."

Idris sheepishly looked down avoiding my stare. Dawn didn't die, she'd just run off with another bloke ten years ago. And here he was comparing the two!

"Sorry Ken.... I didn't..."

I relaxed my stance a bit, and even allowed myself a smirk.

"It's alright, it's alright. My fault. Still a bit raw, you know."

Idris – by now looking at his boots – nervously nodded.

"Hey look, let me buy you a pint. What do you want?" I asked. This instantly cheered him up, and he immediately looked back up at me, absolutely beaming.

"Lovely Ken, yes please. I'll have a pint of Stella."

103

"A Stella, no problem."

'Fucking hell, my wife dies, and I'm buying the fucking pints,' I muttered to myself.

"What was that Ken," Idris enquired.

"Nothing Ken, nothing, on my way now."

That first night, however, I didn't put my hand in my pocket at all – which didn't seem right. Normally people buy you a pint for your birthday, or some other positive news. But then again – being in the chair myself didn't seem right either. I wasn't clear on the etiquette I suppose – it was all new to me. It was a source of disappointment for Ken though, as I didn't even make it to the bar when someone brought one across to me. It was Steely.

We didn't have a bouncer on the door. I don't think the budgets would have stretched to it – but as a community of people, we just policed it ourselves anyway. Anyone coming in looking for trouble, and the whole pub would dive in to protect it, and the regulars. There were some right tasty lads in there too. Steely was probably the tastiest and the first line of defence.

"Hello Ken. I'm sorry butt," he said with a genuine regret evident in his voice.

When the restrictions were lifted in the Summer, and the club re-opened, Steely took a bit more responsibility for the security of our little community. Not only was he the go-to guy for enforcement in our club, but he would now sit nearest the bar door, and even go outside and do short, regular patrols back and forth in front of the entrance to keep an eye out for any police cars – or any other type of officials. He smoked so it wasn't too great an inconvenience, but Mel (the landlord) nonetheless would sort him out with free pints for extra help.

A couple of times I was there when he came bursting in from outside shouting 'Police!' We knew what we were meant to do. It was like when someone stopped the music during a drunken game of musical chairs. Everyone suddenly went on full alert and their eyes scanned around the room to find their 'bubble', and to join them; seated. One or two may have suffered with (alcohol-induced) double vision, and sometimes ended up on the floor instead. Randall cut his head quite badly when in his drunken haste, he completely missed the stool, reached for the table, and pulled it over on top of him. The table somehow missed him - but Dick's prosthetic leg that was resting on top of it certainly didn't. Blood everywhere. Dick said he had to bleach it off his thigh.

The next step was to make sure that they were appropriately distanced. We'd hold the position for a few minutes until (usually) Steely popped his head back in the door and shouted "Clear!" to let us know that the vehicle had passed, and then we'd get back to normal. In the end, no-one ever came in, but Mel always ensured that everyone had a disciplined approach toward this. It was the one thing that came with a 'non-negotiable' clause from him, and as flexible as he could be you wouldn't want to challenge him on this. He was in his early sixties himself now, and had been a publican all his life, but a pub he previously ran for 20 years famously had a boxing ring upstairs in the attic of the building, and this is where he – and others - sorted out many a dispute. It's also common knowledge that he left this pub undefeated. He only left it when they closed it to knock it down and build a block of flats. 90 years old, the building was.

"Appreciate that Steely, thanks butt."

"I was gutted when I heard. I loved Auntie Jan."

Then he hunched up his shoulders, tucked in his elbow on his right arm and poked out his index fingers. He scrunched up his face, and put on a croaky, high pitched Welsh accent.

"*'Steely! You leave those girls alone now. They don't want your germs you mucky boy,'* she'd go!"

He let out an exaggerated, hearty laugh and slapped me on the back – spilling a good third of the pint he'd just bought me all over the floor. He was oblivious – and as his laughing tailed off, he looked distantly into the long since comatose ceiling fan as I shook my soaking wet right hand off and brushed the larger droplets off the front of my shirt.

A few seconds more than was comfortable passed as we just stood there like this, until I asked him: "Been any trouble up here lately has there?"

That snapped him out of it. His detached status instantly passed, and instead his stare shot back down at me and I noticed that he had a big frown across his face.

"Trouble?"

He leaned in closer to me, and in a manner that sounded half like it was a threat, and half like he was imparting a dark secret, in hushed tones, said, "You've seen the fucking size of me, have you?"

I didn't know my back could bend backwards that far, but as he had slowly began leaning in, I had begun leaning back until I ended up at about a 45-degree angle. And we stood stationary in this position for another ten seconds - looking

106

like a close combat battle between Neo and Agent Smith -
until Mel shouted across.

"Steely – go and have a look outside."

Steely stood bolt upright and the dopey smile returned to
his face.

"Alright Mel." he called across the bar, and then looking
back at me said he would see me later, and off he trotted,
pulling his rizlas and tobacco out of his pocket as he went.

Some of the other groups had seen me now. Word had
travelled, and lots of them now came across, one at a time,
to shake my hand and tell me how genuinely sorry they
were. And I could tell that every single one of them meant
it.

Rog and Sal. Rog had a tarmacking company, just him and
his boy. Sal was a hairdresser. We had a cracking New
Years party at their house one year.

Benny and Shaun. Benny had broken his back about 20
years ago when he was a window cleaner and needed
crutches to gingerly get around these days. Shaun – who
worked in the garden centre – was always there to help him
get about.

Linda. I am not kidding – she was smoking hot back in the
day. She would catch the eye of any bloke, and I'd seen it
lead more than once to someone getting a pint thrown over
them, or a handbag across the temple, by their missus. I
think I had been clocked by Jan at least once for it.

Loads of them. Martin and Wendy. Peter and Maxine.
Greg. Paul. Dai Cuckoo. Some of the young – more unruly
– lads that came in there too. I can't remember them all.

I eventually ended up standing alone again and started
drinking the remains of my pint – thinking about going to

the bar to get another one. Not this cheap shit Steely had given me either.

Bugger me, he must have been just stood there, staring at me, and watching me drink the pint I had been given because as soon as I was down to the last swig, Idris came stumbling over.

"Are you off to the bar Ken? Is the offer of that pint still on?"

I rolled my eyes and tutted. "Jesus Christ. Have you been waiting for me to finish?" He was empty handed. "Come on. A Stella was it?" He nodded as he beamed at me.

"KEEENNN-OOOO!"

Someone from the other side of the room called my name which got my attention. There was only one person it could be calling me that. My best mate, Dylan.

"Come over here Ken, I've already got you a pint."

At this news I glanced up at Idris - who looked positively crestfallen – and shrugged my shoulders.

"Don't worry I'll get you one later," I told him, changing directions to go over and see Dill.

"Could I have the money instead maybe K.."

I admit, I shook my head in disbelief and probably was a bit quick to tell him to 'fuck off', but he got the message regardless, and backed off so I could go and join Dill.

It wasn't the first time I had seen Dill since. He had been calling around the house right the way throughout - from when she was in hospital, to the day I heard she was gone. He was my true best mate. As usual, we greeted each other with an embrace and a ruffle of the hair.

"How long you been here? Come and sit over here look. I got us a table."

He motioned me across to a small circular table with two stools at it. It was busy so he had done well, but it wasn't the most comfortable way to sit for a few hours. AND it was next to the gents, which would waft across the stench of piss every time someone either came out of, or went in there, and the door swung closed behind them.

"So how are you Ken?"

"Well shall I answer that how I normally answer it, or.."

"Fuck off Ken, it's me you're talking to now."

I had been reprimanded.

"Well…truth is Dill…," I paused as I took a long swig from my pint. It gave me a second to gather myself before continuing, "Not good. Not good at all."

He solemnly nodded, and I went on.

"I keep coming home expecting her to be there. Keep waking up, expecting her to be there. I keep making plans – but for the two of us. And then I remember."

I glugged down more of my beer as Dill stayed quiet, still nodding at me. I wiped the corner of my eyes. I wasn't crying – it just suddenly felt a bit moist.

"Truth is, I fucking miss her butt. But I know that isn't going to change anything. There'll always be a hole now, and it'll never be the same – no matter what. I'm just keeping going in the hope that there's still enough little positive moments along the way to keep it being worthwhile."

Dill reached across the small table, and put his hand on my left shoulder, giving it a couple of squeezes.

"I know butt, I know. And I'm not going to tell you that it'll all be alright; the hurt will all be over soon. It won't."

We sat there for a few seconds: me staring into my glass, and Dill staring across the table at me with his sympathetic eyes.

"I miss her so much, Dill...I never..."

"Hey – hang on Ken, hold that thought," Dill interrupted, "watch this now."

I looked up into the same direction that Dill was looking, and lo and behold, who was approaching, but Idris.

"Oh what....if he is coming over to ask me for a pint, can you tell him..."

"Ssshhh Ken, no, no. Watch this now," said Dill, with mischief written all over his face.

Idris looked over at us – making eye contact with me – and went by into the direction of the gents toilets. Dill called over and stopped him in his tracks.

"Oh – Idris. There's someone in there."

Idris paused, and looked quizzically.

"Yes – only one at a time allowed in there now look. COVID see. There's someone in there already."

Idris nodded, although the way he shuffled around from foot to foot suggested he needed the facilities quickly.

"I'll give you a shout when it's free," Dill offered.

"Oh, yes please. Thanks Dill," Idris said, and walked back over to the bar – never taking his eyes off the toilet entrance.

Dill switched his attention back to me, and said, "We're all here for you Ken. All of us. Every man, woman or Idris in this club."

We laughed. I looked at him for a moment, and raised my pint, before gently chinking it against his and downing the almost half a pint that was in my glass. I could drink much quicker these days, I found.

The glass hadn't hit the table when I felt the heat of somebody's stare from across the room. It was Idris. He didn't miss a trick. I indicated with my fingers that I would be across to make good on my offer to buy him a pint in two minutes. In the meantime, Steely had come across. Dill spoke up once again.

"Someone in there a minute, Steely boy."

"Never, I'm busting. I'm going to have a piss outside then," he replied, before barging his way hurriedly back through the crowd in the bar, like a White Rhino through a herd of antelope.

I'd had a few pints now, and I felt like I needed to pay a visit.

"Who is in there Dill? They been there ages."

Dill did his hearty laugh and slapped me on the right shoulder – but with more ferocity this time.

"I'm only pissing about – go on, there's no-one in there," he laughed.

"Ha-ha you tosser. I hope Steely doesn't find out."

I got up from the table and walked the few feet to the toilet – the air already becoming thick with the reek of urine – and as I reached to open the door, I could hear Idris calling across from the other side of the bar.

"You twat Ken!"

I looked back and flashed him a middle finger, as Dill was rocking in his seat. Idris was desperate by now, and literally hopping from foot to foot.

"That's two pints you owe me now!"

I did as well a week or so later. When it was just me and him in there one afternoon - about the time we went back into lockdown for two weeks just before Christmas. We sat there talking for about four hours. I didn't realise how dark things had got for him when his wife left him. He completely lost hope. Couldn't sleep. Suicidal thoughts. Even had hallucinations. It triggered him going right to the brink. And he swears that socialising with friends again made the difference. At the Club.

They said she died of COVID-19, but I don't believe it.

We've all heard about how liberally these deaths are recorded. I don't believe COVID-19 was strong enough to take her, but that's what got written down. She had tested positive for a few days after she first went in - but had recovered from it. It didn't make any sense to me.

I keep that to myself though. Well, myself - and a few other people I'm close to.

About forty other people I'm close to.

Waste

What would you prefer? An ear-shaped penis, or a penis-shaped ear?

I resisted the urge to blurt out an answer I would later regret. I'd have to give it some thought – but there was no easy answer, that was for sure.

"Is there a knock-on effect to my decision?" I queried.

Whaddya mean?

"Well, if I had an ear shaped penis, would that mean that my actual ears are shaped in a conventional way? And likewise, if I had a penis-shaped ear, would that that my actual penis looks ordinary?"

Ha-ha…what have we got here? A Ruminating Ronny. A Cogitating Colin. A Pondering Peter. Just answer it - it's a simple fuckin' question!

I genuinely wasn't trying to over-complicate matters and felt a sense of embarrassment overcome me. It was one of his more light-hearted comments, so I had wanted to indulge it.

"I'm sorry Grancha, it threw me."

I cleared my throat a little, and with as much faux-confidence as I could summon, followed up with, "It's obvious now I think about it. A penis-shaped ear."

I imagined Grancha laughing. A deep, guttural scoffing – before the inevitable bout of phlegm-soaked coughing commenced.

And why would you say that?

"Well, having an ear-shaped penis would presumably limit my ability to be intimate with a woman."

I heard him laugh again. A toothless, phlegm filled laugh.

"Well think about it. Before I could get to the stage where that could be a physical obstacle, it is surely something I would need to disclose in advance? I mean, it just wouldn't be right to build a relationship with someone over a period of time, gradually becoming more familiar and tactile with them as the weeks go on, then when the time is right, stimulating this partner into a heightened state of sexual anticipation, only to then throw this almighty curveball their way?"

Go on...

"Whereas I've been fortunate with my follicles, so if I had a penis-shaped ear, then I would be able to grow my hair a little longer and use it to cover my ears."

I see...

"I could use lots of hairspray on it each morning to give it the rigidity it would need to stay in place. I'd make it resemble more of a helmet, than a head of hair."

That could work.

I felt some relief. It was a rare exchange where I'd enjoyed a jovial, light-hearted conversation with the stubborn old bastard. But it would be only for a moment.

Despite my discomfort resting on the aged furnishings, I was able to physically relax somewhat and leaned back into my saggy armchair - its worn through seat betraying the bulges of the metal coils within, that were fighting to penetrate through the fabric like a horde of zombies hypnotically vying for position at the glass doors of a shopping mall, salivating at the thought of ripping into my pale arse cheeks.

It was typical of the furniture in this room. The large oak dresser, the mahogany sideboard, the wall clock with its long since catatonic pendulum. Once upon a time, they were attempts to make a statement about the proprietors' authority and taste in quality articles. Now they sat dusty and dated.

The room had always sat in near darkness. Grancha always kept his curtains permanently closed, but today there was a distinct chill in the room, which was out of the ordinary. I was used to seeing the gentle orange glow from a bulb concealed beneath the plastic mould of fake logs that adorned the base of his gas fire, providing at least the illusion of warmth. But now, it lay dormant and lifeless. I realised I had never seen it turned off before, and I wondered if it could ever be resuscitated.

The TV in the corner of room was normally the only other source of light, and Grancha would sit underneath several old, dog-eared blankets, watching it night and day. When the analogue TV signals were turned off, I got him one that could read digital signals, but he was never confident in changing the channels (not that he would admit it), so since about 2012 it had been permanently left on BBC1 – unless someone like me or Danny came over to see him, and we would change it for him in the event of there being some particular broadcast that he wanted to see.

Danny only came over sporadically, at best. It was mainly just me responsible for all visiting duties. Sometimes the neighbour would knock the door and drop off some Imperial mints, or the last few days newspapers he had finished with. Other than that, it was just the meals on wheels people who he would see. They would let themselves in on weekdays and serve up a decent hot meal in foil trays.

He had never shown appreciation for any these visitors, and I was treated with the same passive-aggression that everyone else was subjected to - but I still couldn't find it in myself to abandon him like everyone else had. Dad hadn't seen his Father for over 20 years – since I was a kid, and when Grancha went way too far that one time. It was hard to deny that he had spent his life mostly being a cruel and twisted man.

So still haven't you got a girlfriend yet? Probably a fuckin' poofter, are you? I know they all make out like it's the fashion now, but they would have had a good fuckin' hiding in my day if they went about like that. And good enough ferrum too!

"People don't really say that word anymore Grancha."

What word?

"Poofter, Grancha."

Well, there's your fuckin' problem right there then isn't it. Everyone pussy-footing around – too afraid to tell the fuckin' truth. To call a spade a spade.

I often wasn't comfortable with the direction these conversations seemed headed in, so I would change the subject.

116

"Has Murray popped in with some papers and mints for you lately?"

Murray? Hah! That old nosey cunt. He's only coming to find out if I'm fuckin' dead yet so he can steal my watch.

There was no way Murray was after his watch, I would think to myself. It could only be of sentimental value to anyone.

"I hope he wears a face mask like the meals on wheels ladies when he comes in here."

Oh, fuck off you soft prick. Load of fuckin' bollocks. Good dose of it – that's what everyone needs.

"You should really insist on it if people come inside the house." This had been a fairly common conversation since around February 2020.

There's no immigrants allowed in my house, so what's the fuckin' problem. They're the only ones you've got to watch.

I sighed. He never disappointed. But it was too late now. When the nationwide lockdown hit in March, he was already 92. His attitude and beliefs system were not going to change now.

He had grown up in the East End of London during the Second World War. After his house was bombed as he and his family had sheltered in an underground tube station, he had been evacuated to Norwich in the second round of evacuations during Autumn 1940, where he'd lived with a family on a small holding. He had told Dad once that it was the first time he had seen real live farm animals, but overall, it was something which he never discussed. I can personally remember him closing down an approaching conversation on the subject by saying something like, "Don't fuck about with the ghosts of the past – you'll only find out they were

117

demons all along." I was too young to read much into it at the time.

He had married my Nan in the 1960's and moved back down to London, having my Dad several years later. He worked at the Wapping newspaper printing press for decades. His shift saw him work through the night, and knock off in the morning, just after the 9 to 5 brigade were clocking in. Like most other working-class men at the time, he liked to have a few pints after work, but in his line of work, it meant getting home pissed just before my Dad would get in from school. I don't know the exact details, but I know there was often violence before he would lurch up the stairs to go to get a few hours kip before he headed out to his next shift. Sometimes being sick along the way.

He came home one afternoon, and my Nan and Dad weren't there anymore. From what I can gather though, his routine didn't change a bit and he never even tried to mend his ways. Or invest any real time in finding them. It had taken Dad to do this when he had become an adult. His Mum had warned him not to bother. He had become toxic, she had said, and would never be any different. He couldn't change.

Dad loosely kept in touch for years, initially out of curiosity and later out a sense of duty, but it eventually fizzled out. Grancha never sent any birthday or Christmas cards – or even took him out for a pint in later years. It was during one visit when Dad took me there in later years that realisation hit him like a blast from the suddenly opened door of a furnace. As impassive as a statue, my Dad just snapped out of it, and realised that Grancha simply did not give the tiniest of fucks about him. And never would.

There's fuck all for you to have mind. You know that do you?

"Yes, I know that."

The council own the house, so they'll be wanting that back. Probably to put a bunch of fuckin' Romanians in here.

This was another well-discussed topic. The destined future use of his house.

Suppose you can have this watch if Murray hasn't half inched it by then. Or the paramedics! Got to fuckin' watch them too.

It was something I never wanted to discuss, but it was typical of his morbid nature to bring things like this up. I would always try to change the subject.

"What are you watching on the TV tonight?"

Something where there's no cunt singing or dancing hopefully.

I had to chuckle at that one.

"Well, I've got to go now Grancha."

Well off you fuck then. No need to rush back. And watch you don't let all the heat out this time.

I glanced around once more as I put my hands to my knees and heaved myself up to my feet. Grancha's house was always bereft of ornaments, or pictures, or anything that made his place seem homely, but I spotted something on the sideboard that caught my attention.

Sat on the corner, in the dim light, I could make out some kind of small sculpture. I made my way over and picked it up.

"You can take that with you mate," called out an unfamiliar male voice from across the room.

119

As he approached, I was able to make him out in the limited light. He was tall and stocky, roughly in his forties. He had a pair of jeans and a white nondescript T shirt on – the oily stains and paint splatters both attesting to the physical work he must have been involved with. Even his face mask looked grubby.

He sidled up next to me and took the trinket from my hand with his black nitrile gloved hands and held it up into the light. It was a small novelty trophy – roughly the size of an egg cup. It had two proportionately large handles protruding from either side and although it once had a silver finish, it had become jaded and no longer shone. It had a small inscription along the small wooden plinth at the base.

"Best Grandad ever. Ha-ha – nice," he said, passing it back to me – before insensitively adding, "Well everyone told me he was a horrible old bastard."

I briefly inspected it, and it sparked the briefest glimmer of recognition within my memory.

"I found this on the floor of the lorry after we had unloaded all his shit into the storage unit. It must have fallen out of one of these drawers. I put it to one side for you in case you wanted it when you came to collect the cash."

"Thanks," I said, still examining the tiny trophy.

"You shouldn't be in here really mate. We have to spray everything with this misting shit to sanitise it before we can punt it on. I don't know why. I told the boss he's already been on a slab in the morgue for over a week but, well, you know how it is at the moment."

I put it my pocket, and took one more look around at all that was left of a mans life. A few pieces of furniture and a dishonourable legacy. It struck me as a selfish, almost meaningless existence, and I felt sad.

"Sorry mate, but I have to hurry you up. I'm flat out at the minute with all these old people dying. Clearing up to 6 houses a day at the minute, making a fortune. Mind you, most of your Grandfather's shit is only good for firewood to be honest with you! Anyway, let me count your cash out."

He pulled a thick wedge of ten-pound notes from his pocket and started counting them out into a pile on top of Grancha's chest of drawers.

"One..." (Embittered soul)

"Two..." (Alienated loved ones)

"Three..." (Heart attacks)

"Four..." (Seasons indoors)

"Five..." (Wasted decades)

"There you go mate. Fifty quid. Sorry for your loss."

Lost

It was only about 4pm, but I reckoned that I had no more than an hour of daylight left. The temperature would plummet then too. Couldn't spend too much longer outside - yesterday evening it had gone down to minus three degrees. It had been cold all day, but I had managed to block it out. My mind was focussed elsewhere.

I was appropriately dressed in a large puffy, Winter coat with a jumper underneath, and a pair of jeans tucked into my boots. I'd give it another couple of hours, but then I'd have to turn it in for the day.

As I took my gloved right hand out of my pocket, I was suddenly aware at just how tensed the muscles in my arms were, having spent the day being persistently driven into the base of each compartment – deep rooted into the furthermost corner; the safest haven that provided the most sanctuary from the biting cold. I stretched my arm out to loosen it up and rotated my wrist in a circular motion a few times. I had a backpack slung over one shoulder with some of my shopping in, and I took the opportunity to switch shoulders.

Raising my hand to my mouth, lowering down my scarf, I pulled at three fingers of my woollen gloves with my teeth – removing the whole glove on the third tug. I placed the back of my index and middle finger against my nose. It was ice cold. So cold, it was at the point where it became difficult to tell if it was extremely chilly, or wet. I needed to wrap this up soon. I had been out since around 8am this morning.

I pulled the glove back on and tucked my scarf back over the lower half of my face. With the (faux) fur-lined hood of my coat worn on my head, there was only a narrow aperture between the various layers of clothing exposed to the cold.

Today had been disappointing. I felt that I hadn't made any progress today, but if I'm honest with myself, that's no different to yesterday, or the day before that. And the several days previous to that each brought with them rapidly diminishing returns, too. In fact, every day since New Year's Eve. It was growing more difficult as the days passed too. It seemed as though I was drifting further and further away with each passing hour.

Early on, Sadies disappearance had gotten a lot of attention on social media. My best friend, Milly, had posted about it heavily on her own page, and shared it in multiple groups on Facebook. In fact, in the first few days, she was posting about it on an hourly basis. Milly had shared her most recent pictures that she had stored in the cloud to accompany the posts too. Unfortunately, most of them were taken when they had been together before lockdown had begun, so there was no definitive way to confirm that they would be up to date. None of her friends had seen her since September, to be able to confirm.

The small, family-owned Italian restaurant she had worked in for ten years had eventually buckled under the pressure of the lockdown restrictions. The unpredictable nature of their industry eventually got too much for the ageing owners, and so they had taken the decision to shut. After investing significant sums of money in new signage, partitions, plastic screens, and all manners of other safety measures – to then see no return due to further changes in the regulations – they had finally conceded defeat and thrown in the towel.

This was a devastating blow for Sadie, which effectively condemned her to the life of solitude that she existed within for the many months that followed.

Her parents were very elderly and had been shielding since March 2020. She had never tried to mask the fact that they never had a close relationship, but I know this still played heavily on Sadie's conscience and had affected her mental well-being over the years.

There is no doubt that their age had always played a part in it. They had Sadie at what was considered to be late in life. They were from a small village, were old fashioned in their ways and harboured attitudes from a bygone generation that was tough for Sadie to relate to. The gap between them was generations apart. I remember trying to comfort her by saying that most parents feel out of touch with their kids - no matter what their age is – but there was no doubt that this was the principal reason she had struggled to bond on any level with them.

They were simple people. The fact that her arrival was a surprise, and completely unplanned was never concealed from her. Her parents already had three boys who were over

20 years older than her, which meant that there was a complete disconnect between her and her siblings from day one. When she had come along, they had already moved out of the family home, and were busy pursuing their own lives, and enjoying themselves socially. This irregular presence of these three much older men in her life, replicated what a relationship with three distant Uncles may resemble. There was never the steady presence of a significant woman in their lives either, which meant that the opportunity for a female role model to look up to within the family unit was just not there at all.

Sadie had always maintained that she sensed as though they felt like they had 'done their bit' for the human race, and that now they should be resting. All the while she was growing up, there were seldom any day trips – unless it suited them. Never any cinema visits. Never any board games. She had never known what it's like to have grandparents (they were all dead), and always described with great sadness how she felt invisible in her own home. Despite this, she would always justify their lack of interest in her to herself by remarking how she always had clean sheets on her bed and food in the cupboard. How could she possibly have any reason to complain?

This would then be contrasted by the increasing levels of guilt that she would feel about these thoughts. They were getting old and felt tired more quickly; and then there were the health concerns. Dad was a cancer survivor, but still needed regular tests and following a stroke when Sadie was only nine, Mum could no longer work. Luckily one of her brothers, Tom, was in the house at the time and thanks to his quick reactions, she had made almost a full recovery. It was the only time she had seen her Dad cry when he arrived at the hospital to visit her - having had the news. She remembered how he had thrown his arms around Tom as tears streamed down his face. His hands tightly had grabbed fistfuls of Toms denim jacket that hung around his shoulder blades as he clung on to him for dear life.

As the only child living at home, they had relied on Sadie to care for her Mum while her Dad still worked, as it happened a few years before he retired. School became a secondary concern for a couple of months, and her attendance became sporadic as she settled into her role as primary carer. Dad set off about 6am for work and got in after 3pm – by which time school was almost over. He didn't do much to help anyway when he did arrive home. I know that she threw every ounce of effort into her new found responsibilities, as she saw it as an opportunity to get closer to her Mum; to build their relationship. Selflessly, she would cater to her every need, but their closeness did not develop the way that she had hoped. She didn't know the word at the time, but later described her Mum's manner as 'utterly apathetic' towards her. As a child, she could not articulate nor understand why she once again simply felt a deep rejection, immediately followed by immense guilt at what she perceived to be inconceivable selfishness on her part. She was caring for her only Mother - who had recently nearly died – and she was worried about a lack of praise for her efforts?

To her credit, she finished school with half a dozen GCSE's and had gone to a local sixth form college. When college was complete, there had been a small graduation ceremony - which her parents had actually attended, showing a small, rare degree of interest - although I personally believe it was just to keep up appearances. It was notable that they were roughly the age of most of her friends' grandparents which had left Sadie feeling self-conscious and embarrassed amongst her peer group. She ran through all kinds of potential nasty comments and sneers in her head, that she was convinced they would be remarking to each other within their social cliques. No sooner had they all left for home, then these feelings gave way to a sense of shame and anger for feeling this way. She would beat herself up relentlessly about it – and blame herself for the distant relationship. "No wonder they don't love me. They're right not to. I'm just a horrible, selfish bitch." I forget the amount of time I would say to her over and over, that she was not to say those things. That she was not being fair on herself. But my voice was small compared to the other voices that were raging inside her head.

And at the epicentre of this roller coaster of perpetual inner conflict lay another real fear – that soon they would die, and she would be left with a crushing sense of loneliness. Although not close, Sadie had remained dutiful and in contact.

One of the reasons that her job had been so important to her was that it partially filled this void. Gianluca, Carmela and Giuseppe were the Father, Mother and Son who ran and were proprietors of the Bella Capri, where Sadie had worked. They had treated her just like part of the family. She always received well-meant words of wisdom and tough love in equal measure from Gianluca, enjoyed girly chats and emotional support from Carmela, and partook in sibling-like competitiveness and light-hearted squabbling with Giuseppe. It had given her the family unit and a sense of belonging that she knew in her heart had been missing.

Of course, it had been a hard year in the hospitality industry, but she had known something was up when she had heard arguing coming from the kitchen one day. Whenever Gianluca and Carmela interacted it was often a lively and animated conversation, ripe with gesticulations, but on this occasion, it had a different tone to it. Over the years she had picked up some Italian, and they had taught her further, eventually gaining the ability to hold down a basic conversation, but on this day, she could not recognise any familiar words they commonly used in the workplace. Except for, 'la Moneta.' The mood felt sombre and was not driven along with the usual expressive passion and zest she was accustomed to.

When Sadie had gone into the kitchen, they had been stood face to face just a few feet apart. When they heard the door, they both instantly stopped talking and jolted their heads to look up at her. Sadie had remembered to me how awkward it had felt. They had continued to go about their business prepping food for the day and cleaning the kitchen down in silence, but Sadie knew she was walking on eggshells from here on out.

Two mornings later, when she went into work, all three family members were stood at and around the bar area, drinking coffee. From their expressions she thought that there may have been a death in the family. Giuseppe never arrived at work before her for a start and such was their work ethic, Gianluca and Carmela were always out the back prepping and cleaning. Once again, her arrival was greeted with silence, as they all looked up at her at once with sad eyes.

Carmela had told her to sit down at one of the tables as the two men remained at the bar area and began staring at their shoes. Whilst the outcome would have been to lose her job either way, the fact that the restaurant was closing its doors completely reduced the level of rejection she would have felt if she were simply being let go. With tears streaming down her face, she had admitted to Carmela after she received the news, that she thought she was being fired. Carmela had grabbed her, held her tightly and they had both cried together over the bistro table.

"Mai! Sei una famiglia," Carmela sobbed. It was the first hug she had experienced since well before lockdown.

The reality of the situation was that despite their promises to continue to see or talk to each other every day, after Sadie had waved goodbye to her surrogate family at the Bella Capri after that last shift, she hadn't seen them again. Carmela had rung several times, but Sadie would not answer her phone. Giuseppe could not locate her on social media, and since she moved flats last year, they were not sure where she lived.

For Sadies part, her acute social anxiety disorder had developed and taken a firm grip on her. Unable to socialise because of the restrictions, estranged from her parents and brothers by this point, and now jobless and stressed out about how she was going to pay rent on her small flat all those feelings of ridicule and rejection had come back to the forefront. The loss of her job, and to her mind, her surrogate family, had triggered her. The unresolved negative events in her life - the trauma, the family conflict – had come flooding back.

She must have sat in her flat, alone, for a couple of months.

The level of social isolation would have been tremendously damaging to someone in her frame of mind. The unrelenting feeling of being alone and divided from others. No connection on any significant level with any other human being. The inevitable deep-rooted feelings of inadequacy and self-loathing.

This presumed period of withdrawal would have done real damage to her. It goes some way to explain what happened the day that her Mother had last seen her. The last day anyone saw her. 25th December 2020.

Her Mum said that the knocking was so slight, she initially had dismissed it. When it became more persistent, she had gone to see if someone was there. The boys had come over for their dinners – two of them were now married and had a couple of kids – and against the national advice they had formed a larger bubble than was permitted. None of them had gotten up to see who was at the door – telling their Mother or Nan that she must be hearing things.

"Oh My God - Sadie? Is that you? What have you done to yourself?"

She put her hands to cover her mouth.

"Why Mum?"

"Why what? Now don't you come here upsetting everyone on Christmas Day. Your nephews and nieces are here, and they don't want you spoiling their day."

Inside the house, her brothers had become aware of a terse conversation taking place in the hallway and tuned in to it.

"Why didn't you love me?"

"Oh, I'm not doing this today. Why don't you come back around in the week? You're not well."

"No Mum. You're right, I'm not."

"Right, I'm going inside. Come up in the week, I'll………My God. What have you done to your hair?"

"I looked after you."

"What do you mean?"

"When you had the stroke - I looked after you."

Her Mother had spoken more softly, sympathetically now.

"I know. And you did a good job and I'm grateful…"

"Then why Mum?"

Her Mother composed herself as this line of deep and personal questioning opened up again. She took a deep breath and stepped back inside attempting to shut the door. Sadie had put her foot in the door frame.

"Get your foot out of my door."

She was an old woman. She didn't have the strength to physically fight it. She called to her sons to come and help.

"Come and tell her to go and stop spoiling our day," she yelled back into the house. Her sons appeared at the end of the passageway.

"WHY MUM?"

"Sadie? What are you doing here? That's enough, you're upsetting your Mother." It was Tom.

Sadie began hysterically laughing. Her Mother covered her mouth, distressed at the forlorn figure her daughter now cut.

"Tom."

"Yes, it's me, Sadie. Look, there's kids in the house. Let's talk in…"

At this point, Sadie had reached out and grabbed her Mother's arm by the wrist. Her boys tried to forcefully remove it so they could bring their Mum inside.

"Ask him. Ask him Mum. ASK HIM!"

Sadie's Mother began to sob, becoming confused.

"For fuck sake Sadie, you're upsetting her, she's an old woman," said Tom as he continued to try to remove her vice like grip on his Mothers arm. Like a banshee, she let out a hellish scream:

"Ask him why he was in the house that day you had a stroke. Ask him what he was doing. Ask him what he was doing to me!"

The adults in the doorway froze and collectively paused for breath, as heads slowly rotated towards Tom. At the bottom of the hallway, a small face appeared.

"Daddy. Can you play with me?"

Sadie released her Mother's wrist and ran off down the street. That was the last anyone had seen her. No one in her block had seen or heard her in her flat for weeks. Her landlord had entered the property with police, and there were no signs that she had been there recently. She had emptied her bank account of the small amount of money in it and left her wallet and phone on the table. The signs had not been good.

I was just arriving at the train station. Pack it in for today – I was cold to my bones. A coffee would help a little.

I queued to go inside the small cafeteria, with all of its seats sealed off with lots of criss-crossed hazard warning tape. Sixth in line, I was happy to wait; it would take a little while to warm up anyway. The cafeteria had adopted a one-way system, with 2 metre gaps, which meant that it looped around the tables in the centre of the room so you could exit the way you came in without getting too close to anyone else.

As I loosened my scarf to breath more easily, I lowered my hood down and ruffled up my hair. It was much more manageable now it was so short, and although I had only bleached it myself over the sink, I was happy with the results. For most of my life I'd had black, shoulder-length hair. Lockdown gave me a chance to experiment. I took my backpack off my shoulder and held it in front of me with both hands as the queue shuffled along.

Out of the corner of my eye, I became aware of a young woman directly across the table that was separating us. She had collected her coffee and was in the process of leaving, but as she had come parallel to me, she had slowed down, before stopping altogether. I fixed my stare straight ahead.

The next thing I knew, the cardboard coffee cup was hitting the floor, exploding upon impact. Particles of the black coffee contained within sprayed three feet up into the air, whilst the rest untidily swathed a circular area on the floor. The immediacy of its presence made it look as though a black hole had instantaneously opened up on the ground - right in front of us.

This unscripted visual provided a fitting metaphor for how the explosion of darkness that I had recently experienced inside me, would look. Without any warning, I felt dreadfully dazed.

I could see that this woman was calling at me, but it was as though I was watching it happen from behind a frosted window. I couldn't decipher what she was saying. The words sounded muffled to me, as though she was under water.

I grew increasingly light-headed and teetered on the spot as I struggled to balance.

She called again, but I was feeling ever fainter. I felt a stranger's hands on my shoulders as they steadied me from behind.

Then the woman was right in front of me. She grabbed me by both biceps and held me firmly. I felt myself coming back around. Her face was so close to mine, I was able to focus more. She looked familiar.

The bag I had been holding fell to the ground and disappeared. I looked down for it, but it wasn't anywhere to be seen. All I could see in front of me was somebody's dirty sleeping bag in its sack on the floor, as I swayed from side to side.

I could suddenly hear words again.

"Look at me! Look at me!"

It was the young woman who had dropped the coffee.

"It's me, Milly. Your best friend. Where have you been?"

As I brought my gaze to hers, I was able to gather myself and a calmness swept over me. With tears in her eyes, she embraced me and held me tight.

"Where have you been? We've been worried sick, Sadie."

And I cried too.

The Death of Dreams

I stretched out my legs as far as I could, raised my arms out up in the air and let out a huge yawn that opened my mouth so wide I thought, for a moment, that it would tear at the sides - giving myself a Chelsea smile.

It was almost midnight and although I normally stayed up late, it was time to give in for today, and head up to bed. It had been a busy week. It seemed as though the shittier things got; the busier work seemed to be. This week at work, we had to plan the close-down of our businesses for another month (at least), send a load of staff home to try and reduce our expense base, and try and get as many of our orders fulfilled as possible before the enforced closure commenced.

At home, Cheryl had just started a new home-based job after her last company was forced to shut, leaving her out of work, and had been busy learning new systems and processes, all the while battling away with the shortcomings of the internet. The kids were full time back in their respective Primary and Comprehensive schools – but the staggered start and finish times meant the doubling of the school runs. And to cap it off, we were also at a reasonably advanced stage of our fostering application.

It was something we had planned to do at some stage – albeit originally, the idea was to wait for our own children to grow up and leave the nest. However, we had decided that now was as good a time as any, and subject to some basic criteria that was important to us, we would take the plunge now. It had involved lots of meetings via Zoom during the evenings, lots of form filling, background checks and interviews – and we knew there would be more to come. And rightly so. But nonetheless, juggling it all was tiring.

We hadn't done anything socially with friends – or as a couple – for what seemed like ages, and it felt like I had accumulated a fair bit of steam to eventually blow off. But so did everyone else I kept reminding myself.

I hauled myself out of the groove that I had vegetated in for the last 2 hours in the compressed corner cushions of our sofa, and swung my feet on to the floor, sitting up. I took in a deep breath and held it there - allowing the air to fill my chest cavity to its maximum capacity, and deliberately flexing the muscles in my left pectoral as I did. I felt the tension there again. It had been there all week, which had been playing on my mind a bit. I hadn't had felt any irregular heartbeats or palpitations, so had tried not to overly concern myself, writing it off as some kind of muscular strain.

I reached for the remote control and hit standby – stopping the 'celebrity' talking-heads filling my screen, dead in their tracks. I found those TV list shows strangely hypnotising – although the amount of crossover moments between them all meant it felt like I had seen them all before. You could guarantee that the same incident from 'Top 100 Embarrassing Celebrity Moments' would show up in the list of 'Top 100 Celebrity Gastric Bypasses'. However, it would give me two hours of what I called 'brain-dead' time – and the requirement to not think at all, sometimes, was welcomed.

Next to me, in her little bed, the dog stirred and opened her eyes, stretching her legs out too as I had done.

"Ready for bed? Come on then."

I scooped her up to take her into the kitchen, where her 'night-time' bed and water bowl was. She was a little Jack Russell called Penny, only a couple of years old, and she would sleep right through the night without making a peep. It was easier the next morning if I let her out one last time first so she could do her business, though. Nothing to clean up.

I flicked the outside light on and looked through my patio doors. The light was not the bright, floodlight type, instead offering a gentle yellow illumination of the immediate area, but it was enough to see that it was not raining outside. If it were raining, even after spending just a few minutes outside, Penny would come with her paws and tummy covered in mud and walk it around the whole kitchen. I would rather clean up the poop in the morning than mop the whole kitchen floor.

"Come on then, let's have a quick pee before bed," I said to her, unlocking the patio door and placing her down on the floor. She immediately ran off a few feet and the darkness enveloped her as she located her favourite spot.

I put my hands in my pocket and stood rigidly – tensing my shoulders to defy the cold. It was the arse end of October now, and getting pretty icy out there. This year had come and gone so fast. I had mostly been continuing with my routine, as I had not stopped going in to work at all, but I felt resentment on behalf of my family. A year had been as good as stolen from them; condemned them to staying at home, aside from some brief interludes when restrictions were relaxed.

It seemed like just last week that I was out here - even at this time of night – stood in a pair of shorts and a T-shirt while the dog did her business. This would affect all the staff who had been placed on furlough this time around. It was great, at first, back in April when the sun was out, and they could all sit sipping gin in the back garden. It was an entirely different proposition now.

For my birthday, my wife had even bought me a wooden bar, with a roof, to go in the back garden. I had gone to work and my Mother and Stepfather had come over and spent the day helping her screw it together. It was fantastic! As well as the storage underneath the bar, she had bought optics, a drip tray, and an ice bucket to go with it. I must admit, it succeeded in surprising me when I got home from work that day – although I had been aware of the presence of freshly cut wood being stored in the garage under a large blanket for the week or so prior, because I could smell it.

The day after it was set up, I bought a large cool box to sit under the bar. When that was brimmed with ice, it cooled the bottles quicker than any fridge. As the summer went on, I added further to it. I screwed metal signs, relating to sport or music, on the wooden wall behind the bar, and I bought two classic wooden bar stools to sit in front of it. With visiting generally limited to outdoor spaces only for the most part, it got a lot of use for several months whilst we entertained safely outside. We celebrated birthdays (other than mine) out there and had a few rowdy evenings with friends - that were probably fairly close to the line in respect to the restrictions, to be honest.

"Penny, where are you?" I whispered, shivering.

I scanned around the garden for movement but couldn't see anything in the darkness. Behind my perimeter fence at the back was a dense woodland which blocked out any streetlamps, or lights coming from the road or other properties. I had some solar powered lights spaced out, each hanging on a single nail along the back fence – but all these did was to give you perspective as to where the boundary fence was, rather than effectively illuminate the area.

I walked along the back of the house to where the alley, leading to the side gate was – adjacent to my bar. A glance down the side demonstrated that Penny was not loitering down there, and I turned around, intending to head back to the patio door and increase the volume of my calls to her.

When I turned, however, I froze. Partly as I was suddenly unsure as to whether I could trust my perception of what I was seeing, and part of it was borne from a fear which had physically immobilised me.

The bar stools, which I would store behind the bar when not in use, to protect them from the worst of any bad weather, were out and set up in front of the bar. The drip tray – hidden on the shelf under the bar whilst not being used – lay out on the counter. There were two whiskey glasses sat on top of the bar with a drink in each of them. The decorative fairy lights draped around the roof and upright pillars – switched off just seconds ago –had flicked on; their faint glow already attracting moths.

As my eyes adapted to this new-found, albeit dim, light source I was sure I could see something else there. Drenched in the darkness.

Did my eyes deceive me?

Somebody - or something - was sat upon one of the stools.

My heart began pounding, and my legs actually shook. I held my breath – too afraid to inhale or exhale – and decided I would silently edge towards the back door. I would get back inside my house, lock it behind me, get the large kitchen knife out of the door, and then go upstairs; maybe speak to it, or warn him off, from an open window.

Firstly, I had to evade its attention, and get to safety.

The first movement I made was to lift my left foot from the floor. Even the sound of the rubber sole of my flip flop being raised off the patio slab seemed amplified. The momentary 'ssshhh' sound taking on far more significance than usual. When it came up completely off the floor, it triggered the rear part of the flip flop to catapult against my heel, making a small clicking noise.

I stretched my leg as far as I could into a side-step before bringing my foot back down. Then, learning slightly backwards from the first step, I tried to repeat this, but even more slowly with my right foot. I glanced back up at the figure that was sat on my bar stool, completely and utterly motionless.

Okay. Stay focussed. Stick to the plan. He – at least I think it was a 'he' – did not seem to have noticed me.

The second side-step with my right foot was flawless. This meant that I now stood just a few feet away from the door back inside my house.

The black shape remained still. So still, I began to think that maybe there was nobody there after all?

I needed to breathe.

I put all my concentration into quietly letting out the air I had stored up inside me moments ago. I took a smaller, shallower breath and readied myself for my next move. I put one hand on the wall for stability and this time kept my eyes on the dark figure.

I knew I was not seeing things. There was something there, and although hard to tell for sure, its form appeared to be that of a large human male. It sat on my bar stool with a hunched back, appearing to lean over the bar on its elbows with its head hanging down. I realised that the stool was barely visible, as it seemed to be wearing some kind of long coat that hung down over its back and almost down to the floor. It looked large too. When I say large, I mean very large. It was tall, and where it was sat hunched, I could see that it's back had a vast surface area, a good indicator of its huge size.

Another few steps and I'd be at the door.

I lifted my foot up aga…

"Why don't you come and join me instead of heading inside?"

I froze again, my heart now beating through my chest. I thought of running but remained rooted to the spot. There was a sudden bumping sound but before I could look down, he spoke again.

"I've poured you a drink."

He spoke in a deep, cigarette and whiskey-soaked drawl. I still resisted responding or moving.

"Come on. I won't ask a third time."

My heart rate – whilst still racing – had become more regular, and almost without thinking about it, I walked slowly towards him.

As I approached, he moved for the first time.

His back straightened up only the slightest amount to allow him to reach across for his whiskey. I was able to comprehend more of the scale of this huge man's frame as his arms, as thick as tree trunks and clad in the sleeves of a long black leather trench coat, reached out with his hand entombed in long black leather gauntlets to grip his glass. To finish this gothic look, I glanced down to see he wore black knee-high boots with metal buckles up each outer side.

If he were to stand up, I was sure he would exceed 7 feet in height.

He moved slowly and systematically, sipping the whiskey before returning it to where it had stood on the bar.

I stood next to him - rigid, awaiting further instruction.

"Sit down."

He didn't say it in an aggressive manner, but it left me in doubt that I should sit down. Strangely, I could not feel my heart racing anymore, at all.

Without looking up still, he said, "Nice bar."

"Thanks. It's really just for friends and family. M-maybe when you've finished your drink you wouldn't mind leaving?" I had to try something, made no sense escalating the situation, so I went with politeness to begin with.

He let out a deep 'hmph' which indicated to me some level of amusement he felt at the comment.

"I poured you a drink. You going to drink it?"

I glanced across to my glass. I had some Jamesons in the optics, it must be that in the glass. Again, wanting to keep the peace, I picked it up. As I held it there for just a second or two, he had seized his glass again, and chinked it against mine before taking another sip. For a big man who had moved so methodically and unhurried up until now, the speed at which he struck now was surprising.

I took a large swig of my whiskey, needing it by now.

I wiped the corner of my mouth, before trying to push him again on what he was doing here.

This time, he let out a huge sigh, and heaved his upper body up straight. His head tilted back, and he looked down his nose and upon me with a scowl. It was the first chance I had to see his face. He had black shoulder length hair that hung lank and greasy from beneath a red bandana that was tied across his forehead. His face was stubbly apart from his chin and mouth area where he sported a short goatee beard. As he observed me from his bulging, round close-set eyes he did not blink; nor stop frowning.

Eventually he spoke again.

"Come on. You know why I'm here."

I took another swig of whiskey.

Confused, I told him, "You know, you look a lot like the American wrestler, the Undertaker."

I doubted he grasped the concept of humour, but although he continued his impassive stare, he did answer.

"Call it 'company policy'. We have a more human approach now. Guess it's the way of the world." He threw

143

his head back as he downed what remained in his glass, returned it to the bar with a slam, and added, "Demise Enablement Officers they call us now."

He pointed at my glass with his gloved right hand.

"Come on, drink up. It's time."

I reached for my Jamesons', ready to savour the spicy, nutty and vanilla tones on the palate, kicking in to the smooth and mellow finish one more time.

Good things happen, and bad things happen. It's just part of the deal. Whatever does happen, you must try and be grateful for. Sometimes more so with the bad things, because of what it leads to cannot be denied. Therefore, it has to be embraced.

The dust always returns to the ground from whence it came.

As I looked across the garden at the house, towards the patio doors, a light flicked on upstairs and I felt a tear roll down my cheek.

My body lay crumpled in front of the patio doors, as Penny cried and howled, licking at my face.

A Request

G G Howells is a Welsh fiction writer with two published works of short stories. 'Narratives From The Lockdown: The Second Wave' is his second book.

If you have enjoyed this book, then please consider leaving a review on Amazon.

If you have any other feedback or suggestions, then they will be gratefully received at the following email address:

info@gghowells.com

Printed in Great Britain
by Amazon